the secret

barb huff

BARBOUR
PUBLISHING

Published by Barbour Publishing, Inc., P.O. Box 719, Uhrichsville, Ohio 44683, www.barbourbooks.com

Our mission is to publish and distribute inspirational products offering exceptional value and biblical encouragement to the masses.

 Member of the
Evangelical Christian
Publishers Association

Printed in the United States of America.
5 4 3 2 1

dedication

For Koni
Thank you for the wonderful poem
and for being such a great writing buddy.
It'll be your turn soon enough.

about the author

Barb Huff leads Moms4Moms, a teen parent support/mentor group through her church. A former youth and family programs director, she lives in northeastern Ohio with her ever-changing family of foster children, her husband, and son.

CHAPTER 1

The strings were velvet under his fingers. With lips locked in bated breath, Parker Blevins gripped the neck tightly in his hand. He could hold this baby for eternity and still not get enough of how perfect it felt against his body. Again, he brushed the surface of the strings. Placing his fingers across the frets, he started to strum a chord.

"You want to plug it in and hear it for real?" a voice behind him asked.

Parker froze, his knuckles white as he gripped the neck of the instrument. For months, he and his friend Elijah Greer had been under intense scrutiny every time they entered Woods' Music Store. More than once Parker had been afraid to even touch the used guitars on the back wall because of the way the owners were eyeing the teens. There was no way he would ever be allowed to touch an instrument like a Gibson Les Paul Voodoo guitar—much less plug one in and play it. This was a serious musician's store.

Dax Blevins clapped his stepson on the back, making him jump again. Parker wasn't sure if he should put the guitar back and look at one a little more in his price range or actually take up the offer to play a fifteen-hundred-dollar instrument. He grinned as he studied the guitar's black body. *Like there are really any guitars in my price range.* Parker was broke in the worst way. He was skipping lunch the next two days just to pay for the picks he needed.

"Sure," his stepdad boomed, "let the boy play."

A look of panic spread across Parker's face at the pronouncement. "Uh, I–I don't know," he stammered. This was a Les Paul Voodoo in his hand—just about the best guitar in the store. What if he couldn't do the instrument justice?

"Nah, play me some 'Stairway,' man," his stepfather insisted, a broad smile of pride spreading across his face.

Parker studied his expression for a moment and thought of Elijah. It was too bad his friend wasn't here to help enjoy this moment. Dax crinkled his face in an exaggerated wink as he folded his arms in anticipation. One of these days, he needed to introduce Dax to his bandmate Elijah. One of these days. . .

"I don't know about 'Stairway to Heaven,' Dax, but I will play something."

Parker pushed a sandy-colored curl from in front of his eye and bit his lip in concentration as he gripped the instrument again. At fifteen years old, nothing had ever felt so right as the wood now melting into his hands. Its shiny black surface screamed, "I belong to you." The music flowed as his fingers danced across the strings. What he was playing wasn't important. The fact that his stepdad—his musical hero—stood inches away from him with captivated attention, eyes beaming, and his arms folded across his chest, wasn't important either. The pureness of the melody filled his soul. The music was all that mattered.

Holding this guitar sent chills through him; it reminded him of the first time he touched an instrument. Parker received his first guitar when he was seven—a bright, shiny student acoustic. Parker felt like he was Stevie Ray Vaughn—"the greatest guitarist to ever touch an instrument," according to Dax. Holding a guitar, whatever the value of the instrument, had made him important. He hadn't known how to play that first guitar, but that fact held little consequence. Stretching his fingers haphazardly across the frets, he would thrash away at the strings as Dax worked with one of his guitar students downstairs in the basement. "In another year," Dax would always say when Parker hinted about lessons.

"You're not old enough yet, kiddo. . .you just aren't focused enough." By the time Dax declared him a fit student, Parker had already mastered a half-dozen chords and could play a number of simple songs by ear. Declaring his stepson a regular prodigy, Dax had beamed.

Dax and his mom married that year, and when his mom insisted that the whole family take Dax's name, Parker and his older siblings Dameon and Corrina didn't argue one bit. Dax Blevins was a local radio celebrity—the evening deejay and late-night social commentator on the largest rock station in the state. "Ultra-cool" being Dax's middle name, all three children were ecstatic to be recognized as part of his family. Dax was known far and wide for offering his opinions in a highly educated fashion every chance he got.

Dameon, then a budding fifteen-year-old musician, bought his first electric guitar right after Dax moved in. Parker soon followed, purchasing his current model at a pawnshop for forty bucks with the earnings from his summer job mowing neighbors' yards.

But to have *this* guitar. . .

The idea of how he would sound—and look—on stage with this instrument in hand sent a new set of chills down his spine. Serious musicians did need serious instruments. Besides, no rocker was complete without a Les Paul guitar.

Parker finished the piece, letting his fingers rest on the strings at the end. What a perfect instrument. It would take forever for him to afford a guitar like this, and he could never accept such a piece of equipment from his stepdad because his parents didn't have that kind of money lying around for frivolous things.

"You like it?" Dax asked, his arms folded. He stroked his fiery red goatee with one hand for what seemed like an eternity.

"Well, yeah," Parker replied, trying to keep the anticipation that was building inside him in check. He rocked back and forth on the balls of his feet, clenching and unclenching his hands in his pockets.

"It's a good instrument."

Parker reeled on the balls of his feet one last time and froze. It felt like every one of his fifteen Christmas mornings had all wound together in his gut. He just wanted to squeal. He knew he couldn't. There was no way Dax would unload fifteen hundred dollars on a guitar. No way.

More importantly, his mom would never let him keep it if for some miraculous reason her husband did buy the thing. She supported her husband's and son's dreams of music stardom, but someone in the family had to be the voice of reason. And she voiced her reasons quite often.

The budget wouldn't allow for a guitar that cost as much as Dameon's car.

"Yeah, it is a good instrument," he mustered through his growing excitement. As much as he tried, he couldn't contain his glee completely. Just the fact that they were actually *talking* about the instrument like it was a possibility was too much for him to keep in.

Dax took the guitar from his stepson and slipped it over his own shoulder. With a sigh, Parker slumped back against the large speaker rack. Even though his stepdad was nearing fifty, Dax's youthful exuberance was evident in his every move. His mane—a much more rusty brown color than his facial hair—hung wildly around his oval face, and his gray-flecked mock turtleneck sweater and fitted black jeans defined his thin body's well-toned muscle. With that guitar in his grip, Dax was the one who belonged on stage with Stevie Ray.

With another wink at Parker, Dax broke into a familiar-sounding riff. Parker recognized the song instantly as one of the classic guitar anthems of the seventies that Dax often played on his radio show. On the *Dax at Night Show*, it was a rare treat indeed to hear a song less than fifteen years old. Dax subscribed to the belief that if a song was new enough to have a video, it wasn't true rock 'n' roll.

Parker spun around, digging his hands into his pockets, and caught a peek at his reflection in the rounded security mirror. His sandy curly hair fell into his eyes. He pushed a curl to the side only to have it fall back into place. "You take an awful long time to make it look like you don't really care how you look," his mom frequently said, and she was right. Between scouring the thrift stores for just the right worn-out T-shirt and twisting each curl into just the right shape, he did spend a lot of time trying to look like he just threw himself together each day. There had always been a method to his madness, however—girls liked a guy that looked like he was just thrown together. But they didn't like the guys who really were.

As every note leapt forward from Dax's fingers, Parker felt the Christmas-morning feeling slip away. They were here to buy guitar picks, not professional quality guitars. Nothing more than window-shopping was going on here. Parker knew the expensive daydreaming was courtesy of his stepdad's fame. Not just anyone would be allowed to take an instrument like that off the wall and play with it. Had it been any parent other than Dax with a teenage wannabe wanting to test-drive guitars, Parker knew they would not be touching that instrument right now.

Another salesman came over to watch Dax play. The greasy-haired twenty-something closed his eyes and let his head drift in circles to the music. As Dax ended his song, the man pumped a fist into the air and whistled. "Dude, that was awesome."

Parker snorted as he held in his laughter. *Can we say, "One too many puffs on the wacky weed?" Find Jesus, dude, and let off the smokes.*

Dax nodded in appreciation and handed the guitar over to the first salesman. Again, he clapped his stepson on the back, giving his shoulder a squeeze. "That's a good instrument, boy."

Parker nodded, tugging at the waistband of his baggy work pants.

"I tell you what. You learn how to play 'Stairway to Heaven' and get that band of yours playing good enough to play in front of an audience, and that guitar will be yours."

Parker froze.

"That's a serious guitar for a serious musician," Dax was saying, but his voice sounded miles away and tin-can-like. "If you're going to be a serious musician, you have to have the right tools, and a Les Paul is *the* right tool."

"Get that band of yours good enough to play in front of an audience, and that guitar will be yours. . ."

If his stepdad knew that Parker's little garage band was pretty familiar with being in front of an audience, what would he think? Having played a dozen times now at different venues, they even had a live demo they cut themselves for sale on the shelves of this very establishment. They still were working to get a professional studio-cut demo. Once they had it in hand, they planned on marketing themselves to recording companies. Their homemade live demo sold so well among concertgoers that they were able to talk the two local indie music stores into selling it. If only his stepdad knew that they were scheduled to headline a local event here in town in less than three weeks. And it was a show that Dax Blevins's own radio station had been advertising for weeks. How could he not be proud that his protégé was really making good on the dream they shared for him?

If only. . .

Parker dug a five-dollar bill from his pocket and dropped it into the clerk's hand.

"What was that you were playing, dude?" the heavy-set clerk asked as he handed him his change.

"I don't know," Parker replied, still feeling dazed. "Something I just made up as I was going along."

"Going with the flow," the clerk replied, an enlightened grin covering his face.

"Yeah, something like that."

"I thought it was sweet, dude. That's what real music is about. The passion behind the creation—not copying some thirty-year-old sorry riff that every stoner knows how to play. No offense to your old man." He scooped the guitar picks up and deposited them into a small paper bag. "That's heart, man."

"Nah, none taken. Thanks," Parker stated, stuffing the bag into his pocket.

Dax was talking to the starstruck salesmen by the door. At the sight of his stepson coming near, he bumped fists with them and excused himself.

What? No autographs today? Parker bit his lip in thought as he climbed into the luxury SUV beside his childhood hero.

He had heart. *But heart isn't going to get me that guitar.* If he wanted that guitar, he was going to have to learn "Stairway to Heaven" and convince his bandmates to give up their ministry for a rock 'n' roll lifestyle Dax would approve of.

Shaking his head at the dated song blaring from the radio, Parker caught another glimpse of his own face staring back at him. A small flyer was taped to the music store's window left of the door. Dax must have not seen it.

"Perfect timing," Dax grinned as he reached for the radio controls and backed the vehicle from the parking lot. He belted out the chorus to the old seventies tune and thumped a fist on the steering wheel to the beat.

Parker's heart skipped a beat—he was sure Dax would see the poster as he turned the wheel and looked back toward the building.

"Isn't that you in that picture?" is what he's going to say, and then what am I going to tell him? "No, no, that's not me. That's some other mop-top kid who plays guitar."

Instead, Dax commented on a Pink Floyd vintage advertisement above it and paid no attention to the local yokel band called Second Rate. Dax considered himself an expert on the local music scene, and a band wasn't anything to pay attention to unless it had *Dax at Night's* seal of approval. A group of kids who tacked their own poster up in a window wasn't worth his time.

Focusing on the trees lining the street, Parker sighed in relief. Convincing his friends to start worshipping sex, drugs, and rock 'n' roll would be much easier than explaining to his stepdad about being in a band that sang the praises of the forgiveness, love, and mercy only found through Christ Jesus.

Dax wouldn't go for that at all.

CHAPTER 22

The wave of heads pulsing to the music in front of the stage brought a smile to Parker's face. This was by far their largest crowd since they had started the regular gig at Plaza Java. People were stacked on top of each other on the dance floor and spilled over into the sitting areas. They jumped in unison—a cascade of motion all to the beat of their instruments. He was glad to see that as each performance went by, their crowd got younger and younger. Second Rate's music was supposed to be for their peers—not the youth pastors and young adult Bible study groups that frequented the coffeehouse with a goal of Christian outreach. He didn't mind when they came, but he wanted their real support coming from his own age group.

Seeing so many teens out there set the bar even higher. Maybe they really were doing something bigger than music.

Thrashing his head along with the crowd, he turned his attention back to his strings. The old guitar was still rocking 'em out. Who needed a Les Paul Voodoo anyway? He was playing for God. And his old no-name brand did just fine by this crowd's standards.

"I didn't know where I was. I didn't know who I was, 'til I found You." He shouted the words to finish off the song, squealing the chord in protest as the music ended abruptly.

The crowd roared in approval. The punk anthem penned by their lead guitarist Darby McKennitt always brought the most response from the audience.

Parker let his guitar hang limp from his shoulder as he clasped both hands around the microphone. Giving the crowd time to fall into a hush, he closed his eyes. This was his favorite time of the show—leading a room full of strangers in a prayer that united them into one body, if only for a few brief moments. "Abba," he whispered into the microphone, "my Father. I didn't know I was lost until I realized You were searching for me. I thought I knew who I was until You showed me that I was nothing without You. Father, You made the heavens and the earth." His voice cracked heavy with emotion. With a deep breath, he regained his composure. "And yet You concern Yourself with something as insignificant as me, Lord, as if I were the only thing that mattered to You. I am so unworthy, Lord, but You love me. I praise You. Lord, we praise You."

He lifted his hands in the air as the guitarist perched on a barstool beside him started a slow, melodic riff. "Lord, we praise You," he said again.

A sea of hands reached up as Parker turned and smiled at Darby McKennitt. Her face was buried beneath the hair swaying in front of her eyes as she continued the melody. Darby's twin, Andria, crossed her drumsticks quietly across the snare and crept from behind the percussion section into the narrow shadows beside the stage. The other members of the band exited as well.

"We praise You."

As he followed the others, Parker whispered the words again, and the stage went dark.

A hand rested on his shoulder as he stopped near the stage. He reached up and grasped it tightly. He knew who was reaching out to him without seeing her face—Shanice Stevenson was a longtime friend. His bond with each of the members of the group was unbreakable, but with Shanice the connection was special. There was such a frailty and innocence to the thin tomboy who wore her hair in multiple braids. Parker felt as if he had to protect her from the world that she seemed oblivious to most of the time. From day one at the elementary school they both attended, he had looked after her. As far as he was concerned, the other girls in their band were the friends that he would treasure forever. But this girl with the round hazel eyes and caramel-colored skin was the baby sister he would never have.

A spotlight warmed the floor as Second Rate's lead singer, Jenna Rose Brinley, walked to center stage. Darby continued with her guitar playing as the light softened on both of them.

"Can you believe this crowd?" Shanice whispered near his ear.

Parker shook his head. Inside, he wanted to hush his friend. Didn't she see this moment was a close second in his "favorites department"? Jenna Rose was beautiful. He loved the way her blond hair framed her face and how her eyes sparkled in the rose-tinted light. Her white baby doll tee displayed tiny rhinestones at the neckline, and her flare-legged jeans had threads of sparkly material woven throughout. She looked fantastic. Most of all, Parker loved the sound of her voice. There couldn't be much on this earth closer to the songs of angels than Jenna Rose's voice.

"Do you need a drink?" the other guy in the band asked. "Hey, space boy!"

Parker turned his attention to the tall, skinny teen clad in red plaid pants and a black T-shirt—the bass guitarist and his best friend, Elijah. "What?"

A lighthearted snicker escaped Elijah as he shook his head. "Man, you are sorry."

"Just throw me a bottled water."

Elijah tossed him a water and closed the lid on the cooler. "Would you just ask the girl out already?"

"Man, booger off, will you?" Parker tried to say lightly, but the words echoed in his head.

Man, that show was so sweet," Elijah mused as he twisted the extension cords around the crook of his elbow. It was three hours after they had taken the stage, and the room around them had emptied save the few employees cleaning and the band members wrapping up their equipment.

Parker pumped his head in agreement. "I love performing! I'm on such a high the rest of the night. I hate to step off that stage." Wiping his palms on his baggy jeans, he scooped up his guitar and Darby's in their cases and stepped into the warm night air.

Chance McKennitt's van took up the entire width of the alley between the coffee shop and the vendor next door. The aged vehicle Second Rate used had one red door with rust spots which somewhat matched the rest of the van's rusty blue body. Stickers proclaiming Chance's faith and also his love for Christian music littered the back bumper. It wasn't the prettiest set of wheels on the street, but without it and the twins' cousin, the band would be little more than a group of kids with big dreams still stuck making noise in the back of a little pizza shop.

Elijah followed Parker's lead with his arms full of audio equipment and microphone stands.

"You work tomorrow?" Parker asked.

The tall boy with the stubble appearing all over his head nodded and tossed the cords in the milk crate where they belonged. Elijah worked for his uncle's pizzeria on the weekends and after school. "What you got in mind?"

"I don't know. Hang out doing something," Parker replied. "Darb and I were going to work on the music for that new song at Amber's house in the afternoon. You could come over, too."

Elijah returned to the building with his friend in tow. "Sounds cool. You know I don't read music though. I'll probably just get in the way. You guys write it, and I just show up to play it."

Parker laughed as he watched the other boy cross the room where the rest of the band members were lounging on the overstuffed furniture in the side room of the coffeehouse. "Dawg, I hardly read music, but that's not stopping me. I don't know how it's being done exactly, but Darb and I are coming up with some sweet music."

"I might pop over," Elijah replied. "Probably I'll just get in the way though."

Dismissing him with a wave of the hand, Parker grabbed the last speaker and headed outside. Elijah knew a lot more than he liked to let on. For him, playing dumb was a good defense mechanism.

A slight breeze blew warm on his face as he rounded the corner, the scent of an impending summer storm a soft kiss on his cheek. Parker drew in a deep breath and closed his eyes as he thought of other warm summer nights. This was the kind of night he and Dax would sit on the back porch playing chords and watch the lightning split the sky. Chugging sodas, they would draw in deep breaths of the humid, musty air and try to outlast one another, ending their contests with carbonated-induced belches and laughter.

Mom, who was usually sitting inside at the kitchen table, would call them gross and tell them they needed to stay out there if they were going to be pigs.

Sometimes Parker's older brother, Dameon, would join them, but lately, he hardly picked up his guitar. His brother, a twenty-four-year-old college graduate, seldom did anything of late. Mom suspected he was smoking weed, gaining that idea from a television commercial that focused on that topic, but Parker knew his brother's current reticence had nothing to do with drugs. Dameon Blevins was single after being half of the hottest couple on campus for three years, and Parker knew his brother felt like a failure because of the breakup. That situation, coupled with the fact that Dameon was currently lining up cereal boxes on shelves on his late-night shift at the local grocery store while his college diploma gathered dust on his bedroom wall, was a major blow. One college roommate was driving a BMW and the other was currently in medical school. And then there was Dameon, who was mailing out resumes from his mom's living room. Sometimes, Parker thought it was a miracle his brother wasn't doing drugs.

Parker hefted the last of the equipment into the back of the beat-up van and pulled the hatch closed. Beside the van, two girls waited with Second Rate's CD in hand. He hadn't seen the two girls coming. "Hi," he stated, surprised. "Wow. Where did you come from?"

"Hi," they said in unison, as if they had practiced it repeatedly to get it right.

"It's not nice to sneak up on people in a dark alley this late at night." He ran his hand through his hair and took a deep breath. Flashing a big smile, he added, "Let's try this again. Hi. Were you at the show?"

The girl with a short, spiky hairdo similar to his friend Andria's smiled and shuffled her feet a bit. "It's Parker, right?" she asked.

He nodded. "And you are. . . ?"

"Janet," she replied, throwing a thumb toward her taller friend with the long red hair. "This is my friend Tamara."

"Did you enjoy the show?" he asked the girl introduced as Tamara. He stuck his hand out to greet each one of them.

"Yeah," Janet replied, rocking on her heels. "You really rock. You have the most intense eyes I've ever seen." She grazed a hand across the side of his face.

"Um, thanks," he muttered, stepping back from her.

"Can you, like, sign my CD?" Tamara asked, thrusting the plastic case at him. She pulled a permanent marker from her pocket.

"Oh, sure, of course," he replied. He scribbled his name in the best nondescript handwriting he could muster. "Let me get the rest of the band out here for you."

"Nah, that's cool," she replied, popping her gum.

"Yeah," Janet replied, stepping closer to him. She placed the CD in his hand, letting her fingers linger across his for a brief moment. "You're the cute one. Will you sign mine, too?"

Parker tried in vain to keep the smile from crossing his face, but it crept around the corners of his mouth and brought a sparkle to his eyes. "Now, come on," he replied, pointing back toward the stage door. He could hear Elijah's laughter from inside. He scratched his name on her CD cover and handed it back. "You know you want everybody's autograph. You *need* everybody's autograph. Make the CD more valuable someday."

"Nope," came the answer from them both.

My goodness, ladies. Please tell me you aren't here just to flirt with me because you're looking rather trashy. Shifting his eyes back to the door, he contemplated how he could persuade the two fans otherwise. This band wasn't supposed to be about any one of them, and he didn't want to do anything that might upset his buds. Then again, these were fans who were showing an interest in what they were doing—how could he tactfully turn them away?

"This your first Second Rate show?" he asked, trying to turn the focus back off him.

Janet nodded. "A friend hooked us up. Didn't have anything better to do on a Saturday night."

"What church you go to?"

"We don't really go to church," Janet replied. Parker noted that her demeanor had turned defensive as she stepped away from him and stuffed the CD in her bag. "At least I don't."

"I go to a youth group now and then," her friend added. "It's okay, I guess."

Parker smiled, gleeful that he had taken control of the situation again. "We go to Faith Calvary Temple. You should come over and check it out sometime. We have a youth service Sunday nights."

"What are you doing now?" Janet asked, cocking her head sideways in a flirtatious way that Parker bet she had spent a lot of time perfecting.

"Yeah," Tamara continued. "So we have this party we're heading to—"

Parker shook his head and stepped back from the girls. No parties. No girls. He needed to get back inside before he found himself agreeing to things he didn't want to agree to anymore. "Thanks, ladies, really," he said, making his way to the door. He stopped at the entrance and turned to face them. "Thanks for coming and all. I hope you enjoyed the show, and I'd love to see you stop by church, but I can't make it tonight."

"It's just a thing at a friend's house," Janet pleaded. Her voice wavered as if she wasn't used to hearing the word no and wasn't sure how to respond. "It's totally innocent, I swear."

"We're good Christian girls." Tamara's voice was thick with sarcasm. It was all Parker needed to hear as he closed the door.

CHAPTER 4

The coffeehouse was nearly empty as Parker fitted the chain lock around the door handles. He flipped the stage lights off and made his way to the counter. The two girls were still standing in the alley. Guilt washed over him for leaving them outside. Shaking off the feeling, he sidled up to the counter. Probably they would be just fine; after all, they had found their way into the alley on their own—they were capable of finding their way back to their car without his help. It wasn't a bad neighborhood or anything. *Deny it all you want, pal.* Parker admitted somewhat ashamedly that if he would have stayed and talked with the girls any longer, his old self just might have won out. That was the real reason he had come back inside. Parker wanted his old self to stay buried.

"I already ordered you a caramel latte!" Jenna Rose called out. She pointed to the clear glass mug resting on the end table beside her.

Flashing a smile at the girl behind the counter, Parker joined his friends in the cozy sitting area. Squeezing beside Jenna Rose in the oversized easy chair, he thanked her for the coffee and took a long sip. Its sweetness warmed his throat, but as it went down, hunger grabbed at his middle. "Everything's in. Thanks for all your help, guys." A playful note of sarcasm bit at his words.

"Anytime," Andria replied. She was sitting on the sofa with her legs stretched over her sister's and Elijah's legs, her sandals lying on the floor in front of her.

Unable to resist, Parker grabbed her foot, nearly spilling his coffee in the process. As she wiggled and howled in laughter, his tickling grew relentless.

"Say 'Parker is my hero,' " he demanded.

She turned and twisted, refusing to concede. "Never!"

" 'Parker is my hero.' Say it."

With one swift push, Darby sent her sister flailing, though Parker held onto her foot. Relentless, he kept his grip and tickled her harder. Andria tried to steady herself against the coffee table, but she still landed on the heavy braided rug. "Get off my feet," Darby said through her laughter.

"I won't say it!" Andria squealed, trying with all her might to release herself from Parker's grasp. "Somebody help me!"

The others roared in laughter around her, cheering on Parker's antics.

Parker continued tickling her feet. "Then I won't stop. Come on. 'Parker is my hero.' Say it. Say it!"

"Never, never, never!"

Just as quickly as he started, he stopped. The game wasn't fun any-more—Andria was right. She'd just as soon wet herself than actually give in to a demand like that. Nobody got Andi McKennitt to do some-thing she didn't want to do. If she said she wasn't going to say uncle, then she wasn't going to say uncle.

He plopped back down into the chair and wrapped his arm around Jenna Rose's shoulders. She comfortably snuggled into his side. Parker bit his lip, letting his nostrils flare as he caught his breath. Not for the first time, he wondered why she did that.

Probably for the same reason you put your arm around her, dork.

He knew he probably should pull away. Maybe even go sit some-where else. There wasn't really enough room in the chair for the both of them anyway.

But being so close to her felt so right.

Besides, they were just two buds hanging out with the rest of their friends, he reasoned. What was the harm in getting comfortable in the small chair? Where else was he supposed to sit?

He could put his arm around Shanice or Darby or Andi and not wig out over the implications. It was harder with Jenna Rose. He drew in another breath, her pleasant scent lingering in his nose, and nodded. Jenna Rose Brinley was his friend. Friends showed each other love, and he could put his arm around her without it leading to anything more than that. He really could.

Dude, you're thinking too much. You're sitting by the girl, not proposing to her!

"I'm starving," he blurted to the others. Time to change the subject in his head. "How 'bout we go find something to eat?"

Darby grabbed her stomach. "I'm stuffed. Dad was home for the first time in weeks, so we went out to dinner before the show. It was awesome, guys. I don't think I've ever eaten so much. But best of all, they were actually talking and stuff." She glowed with happiness as she shared the news.

"Wonders never cease," her sister grumbled. "I could use some cheesecake. I don't care how much I ate at dinner. There's always room for midnight cheesecake runs," Andria added.

Parker noticed the twins had avoided looking at each other during their conversation. It was no secret among their group that the family that sat in the third pew at church every Sunday was not the *real* McKennitt family. Parker wondered if anyone really understood what exactly did go on behind their door. Their dad traveled regularly on business trips, but things seemed cold between the married couple when they were both in town together. Neither of the girls opened up much about the whole situation, but they also didn't try to hide the fact that the ride wasn't very smooth.

"Hear, hear, sister," Shanice said, downing the last of her mocha. She set the mug on the table behind her and stood up from her seat. "I am all over that cheesecake. Let's go. Dinner was a long time ago."

Amber and Elijah also jumped up.

Parker looked down at the pretty girl curled up against him. His stomach rumbled and growled as hunger tried to overthrow his heart, but he didn't want to move. This—them—was just too perfect. He didn't want to move.

Too bad they don't serve sandwiches or something here.

Jenna Rose looked up at him with a similar reluctance coming through.

"I could eat," she said. "But no pizza. Like a Denny's or something works for me."

"Well," Chance chimed in, "let's get moving then."

Parker looked at the college guy sitting backwards in the hardback chair next to the sofa. Their eyes locked momentarily. . .and Parker to detected an uneasiness in Chance's voice.

Was that jealousy in his eyes?

CHAPTER 55

Parker made a point of climbing in the front seat of the van. Jenna Rose paused, wrinkling her brow in concern. He could imagine what she was thinking since they had always sat beside each other on van trips. Raising his eyebrows, he smiled at her and winked.

Trust me, Jenna. I think it's best for both of us. Sometimes he had to protect himself from himself.

She looked hurt as she settled into the backseat beside Amber. With a quick glance in the mirror on the sun visor, he watched her scoot into the seat and fiddle with her bag until Elijah sat in the other row and blocked his view.

Chance turned the key as Shanice pulled the sliding door closed. The van roared to life. Pulling his seatbelt around him, Chance motioned for Parker to follow.

"We about ready to cut that demo?" Parker asked as they started down the alley. The van sputtered and lurched as it navigated the narrow roadway.

Any kind of conversation was good to Parker's way of thinking. If they talked about the band, he didn't think about how much he liked having his arm around Jenna Rose.

Chance nodded, his voice filled with a cautionary tone. "I think we should go in with the cash for at least ten hours in the studio. We need about three more gigs to get there."

Parker stole a glance sideways at the college guy who had found his way into the group in a managerial role. Chance was scowling, his eyes fixed intently on the road ahead and his mouth wrinkled in thought. This guy was no teenager anymore, but he was hardly a man either. Parker knew the longing in Chance's eye when he saw Jenna Rose enter the room—it was the same feeling Parker himself was trying to suppress.

Jenna Rose was fifteen years old.

Parker stretched his neck to the side so he could turn his head toward the rear of the van. Elijah, forever a pal, leaned sideways so Parker could make eye contact with the blond in the backseat.

She smiled when she caught Parker's eye on her and twitched her nose playfully.

Yeah, she's practically a baby. Too young and innocent for either one of the two of us in the front seat of this vehicle, that's for sure.

"Why ten?" Shanice asked from the back. "Do you really think it's going to take that long? We're going to record what? Eight songs at the most?"

"Well, I've never recorded a demo before," Chance admitted as he drove the van through an empty downtown intersection. "I just want to be a bit conservative. I want to see your first demo be good enough to get you where you need to go so you don't have to spend the money to record another one."

Elijah agreed. "I don't want to be in the middle of recording and run out of money. When we make our next CD, they need to be paying us."

Parker turned around and high-fived his friend in agreement. "Definitely!"

Leaning over, Parker flipped the van's radio on. A familiar voice flooded the airwaves. "Hey," boomed the deejay that happened to be his stepdad. He was using his radio personality voice as Dax liked to put it. Parker hardly noticed a difference in the two voices of his stepdad.

"Check this Z-fans," Dax addressed his audience. Papers rustled in the background. Parker knew this meant he was going to go off on one of his tangents. Dax always had to make sure he had his facts right in front of him before he would say a word on a situation. "The annual Fourth of July downtown block party will feature the sounds of local Christian band Second Rate. . ."

"Did you hear that?" Shanice leaned over and pounced on the radio dial, turning the sound up. "They just mentioned us on the radio!"

"Yeah," Andria said skeptically. "*Dax at Night* just mentioned us on the radio. That's not a good thing. We're about to get trashed."

"My sources have uncovered the fact that this so-called 'entertainment' has a religious-right agenda," Dax began. Parker could hear the fervor in his voice. Dax was only warming up. The best—or as Parker saw it, the worst—was yet to come. "Can someone tell me why this city's governing body not only hires a religious act as entertainment but also goes to great lengths to hide the fact that this group has such an agenda?"

"We have an agenda?" Jenna Rose echoed from the backseat. "If he was talking about anyone but us, this would be funny."

"What are we hiding?" Shanice added.

Andria studied Elijah's look and then her own before she smacked Parker on the elbow. Andria's hair, currently dyed black, stuck up in crazy spikes all over her head. Her earlobes were covered in piercings, and her makeup was as dark as her T-shirt, which sported the word "Freak" across it. Parker pretended to flinch and turned to look at her. Pointing to herself and then Elijah, Andria laughed. "Now we sure look like members of the religious right, don't we?"

"We're the secret punk brigade," Elijah added. For good measure, he pushed up his square-framed glasses with one black-painted fingernail.

"The punks of the religious right!" Andria fell into a fit of laughter as she rolled onto the floor of the van.

"Be quiet," her sister scolded, poking Andria's shoulder with the toe of her shoe. "I want to hear what he's saying."

"Why? He's an idiot."

Parker wanted to melt into the back of the seat, but he also wanted to hear what his stepdad was saying. "I want to hear, too."

Andria clawed her way back on the bench seat and buried her head into Elijah's shoulder, trying to suppress the giggles that kept coming. They all turned their attention back to the radio.

Closing his eyes, Parker could see Dax behind his desk, masses of jumbled wires sticking out of machines and the computer screen in front of him, a WZFM coffee mug cooling at his side as he ranted. His caller board was probably glowing in all colors, and he was ignoring those faithful listeners while he broadcast his opinions. Dax was known to keep callers on hold for hours while he let others who shared his opinions talk for much longer than other radio call-in shows would allow.

"Taxpayer money goes into this city event. My money. Your money, friends. Tell me, did you ask for your money to be used to be preached at unknowingly on a Saturday afternoon?" Dax asked over the airwaves. "Singing 'hallelujahs' with your kids instead of groovin' to some good ole rock 'n' roll? I know that's not where I'm wanting my money to go. I want a public event that celebrates our community as a whole and doesn't shove someone's agenda down my throat. That's what I want. You can't tell me that of all the fantastic local music available out there the best they can do is a lousy Christian band. Mark my words, friends, this is about more than music."

"Man," Elijah said with a sigh as they entered the restaurant parking lot, "if he takes our biggest gig away from us. . ."

"It's cool," Parker shot back. "We're not losing our gig."

As he bit his bottom lip, Parker banged his head against the seat. Dax Blevins always had a plan of action when it came to the idea of religious/civil issues. He lived for this kind of stuff—righting the wrongs of the system when it came to the separation of church and state.

Parker needed his own plan. . .quick.

CHAPTER 66

They poured from the van into the thick night air. The breezes from earlier had ceased, and the sky hung heavy with an impending downpour. A half-dozen cars dotted the parking lot, and a heavy buzzing noise came from the half-lit restaurant sign.

Parker stood at the door and offered his hand as Jenna Rose stepped from the vehicle. "Hi there," he said with a smile.

"Huh, do I know you?" she replied, climbing out without his help.

"Ouch, she dogged you!" Elijah whistled.

Parker grunted as he shoved his friend and closed the van door. "She'll love me again in a minute," he cracked, flashing his bright green eyes at her.

"Doubtful," Jenna Rose retorted, spinning around and placing an arm around Andria's shoulder.

Doubtful? Right.

Hurrying across the parking lot, they entered the building just as the clouds opened up.

The disheveled hostess emerged from the kitchen, wiping her arms on a dish towel. She glanced over the large group with a sigh and scooped up an armful of menus. Mumbling something about curfews and the late hour, she led them past a long booth full of teens to an empty group of tables at the back of the restaurant.

Parker's heart skipped a beat at the sight of the laughing circle of friends filling the booth. He recognized a girl who was clad in a skimpy T-shirt and wearing too much makeup immediately. The redhead named Sierra was a friend of Parker's sister. Another girl and three boys filled the table, a half-eaten plate of hot wings in the center, but they were not the ones he was hesitant about spying him.

Lord, don't let her see me.

Ducking behind Elijah, who was taller, Parker hurried to the empty table and grabbed a seat on a bench with his back to the other party.

The last thing he needed right now was to deal with Sierra. Jenna Rose bumped against him as she slid across the bench. With a smile, she scooted to the center as Darby took the last seat on the bench.

"You over being mad at me yet?" he asked, trying to keep his voice barely above a whisper.

As she tucked part of her hair behind her ear, Jenna Rose grinned. "I don't know. Should I be?"

Parker wrinkled his nose and bumped her with an elbow. "How can you still be mad at me? Aren't I too cute for that?"

"I'll think about it," she replied. Darby was asking her something, so she turned her attention toward the conversation happening on that end of the table.

Parker slunk down behind his menu, pondering his next move. Sierra, a senior like his sister, and Corrina had been inseparable for most of their lives. They were both boy-crazed music freaks who worshiped the boy-band-of-the-month from fourth grade on. Both of them had a penchant for guitar players, and Sierra had gleefully discovered that her friend's kid brother was into girls who were into guitar players. The summer before Parker entered high school, she set her sights on the curly-headed skateboarder with the blue green eyes and electric smile. Her overnighters increased, and Corrina always seemed more than happy to head to bed early, leaving the two of them alone together in the basement's finished rec room.

Parker squeezed his eyes closed until his cheeks hurt, drew in a deep breath, and opened them. Those days were long gone. Those were

BC days—before Christ—that he didn't want his new group of friends to know about. If Sierra spotted him, then he might have to do some explaining.

"You okay?" Jenna Rose leaned over and whispered.

He nodded. Man, she smelled good.

"Okay," she said, drawing the word out as if she didn't fully believe him. She turned her attention back to Darby and Chance at the other end of the table.

Having her nearby definitely didn't make things any better.

Two hands slid under his menu, which had enclosed his person behind its three walls quite nicely. The menu was lifted from the table. A bit startled, he shrank down farther into his seat and then smiled as Shanice's face came into view.

"I don't think she saw you," his friend whispered. She laid her chin on her hands, resting the menu on the table. "You can breathe."

How does she know? "Who?" he asked, his voice cracking more than he would have liked as he said the word.

"Don't play dumb with me, Parker. I saw her, too. I remember the way she used to look at you."

His heart was racing right out of his chest. Of course, they all had to know *something* about his past reputation—they did all go to the same school. But he always thought that maybe the stories hadn't gotten to them since they were more likely to avoid the rumor mill than most teens. He would have liked to believe they all walked away when rumors about his past surfaced. Or maybe they were too busy with evangelizing or analyzing the latest Christian tune to listen. But judging from her comments, Shanice might know more that he thought she did.

"When?" Parker glanced at the others to see if anyone else was paying attention to the quiet conversation they were having. They all seemed to be engrossed in their own discussions and were not paying attention.

Whoa. How much does Shanice really know? We've been friends forever and all, but does she really know about Sierra and me?

His stomach jumped to his throat. Sucking in a breath, he clamped his mouth shut.

What else does she know about me?

"I need to go to the bathroom," Parker said, realizing immediately afterward that he had spoken loudly. The other conversations came to an abrupt stop as all heads turned to look at him. Even the waitress stopped, pen in mid-air. She cocked her head, and her brow wrinkled in confusion.

Darby jumped up to make room for him to slide out of the bench seat. "You okay, Parker?" she asked as Jenna Rose scooted out of the way next.

Parker nodded as he tried to stand up. He stopped as his eyes caught sight of the back of Sierra's head. The other girl at her table held his gaze for a moment and then leaned forward to whisper to her friend. Parker lurched backward, nearly falling on the floor. He wondered if this other girl knew who he was. "False alarm," he mumbled, shaking his head.

"Nice move," Shanice retorted as the others turned their attention back to the waitress and resumed placing their orders. "I'm sure if she didn't see you before, she did now."

"What do you know about her?" he asked after scrutinizing Shanice's face for some sign.

"Back when we were still allowed to skate in the park," she replied, "that girl used to watch you. And I mean *watch* you. She wasn't just hanging out to see some air or something. You could tell that chick was into you." Shanice straightened her shoulders and crossed her arms on the table. "And I remember how you used to look at her, too."

Leaning forward, he scanned his friend's face again for some sign of how much she really knew. Was she just talking looks here? Or did she somehow know how far his relationship with Sierra had gone?

"What can I get you, honey?" the waitress asked in a tired, ragged voice.

Suddenly he realized he had never even looked at the menu.

"What? Oh, hot wings, with lots of blue cheese and extra celery."

"And to drink?"

"Uh, water is fine."

A good night's sleep never sounded so good. And he really did have to go to the bathroom. Banging his head lightly on the table, he sighed again. But leaving wasn't an option until Sierra was gone. Being anywhere but here would be good right about now.

It could be worse. She could come over here and want to talk about the good old days.

Stealing a glance over Darby's shoulder, he could see that the waitress was scribbling something on her notebook at their table as well. She was ordering ice cream. He remembered then that Sierra always had ice cream when she was out.

"Just leave already, will you?" he whispered, smacking his forehead on the table.

"I don't see the big deal," Shanice exclaimed. "It's over, isn't it?"

Parker shot her a dirty look. He knew Christ now. He wasn't that person anymore—or at least, he tried really hard not to be. Sometimes he failed, but not with something as big as this. There was nothing inappropriate going on in the Blevins' basement rec room anymore that involved him, thank you very much. "Of course it's over. How long have you known me, Shanice?"

"What's over?" Andria queried as she passed Parker his glass of water.

"Nothing."

"What's over?" she asked again, turning her attention to Shanice this time.

Shanice took her glass and shook her head. "Old news. No big deal."

Andria didn't look convinced. "You two have been gabbing about something that sure doesn't seem like nothing."

"Honest, Andi," Shanice replied, stirring sugar into her iced tea. "It's nothing."

"What's nothing?" Darby asked, turning toward the conversation. Soon they were all asking the same question. Shanice looked longingly at Parker for any answer to set them all at ease.

"I wrote a song," Parker blurted out.

I did what?

"You wrote a song?" Darby leaned forward onto her fist. Those were always the right words to get their songwriter's attention. "That's so cool, Parker! I knew you had it in you. Tell us about it."

Stealing a helpless glance at Shanice, he stammered, his head racing for a theme that would be suitable. She just raised her eyebrows and smiled at him with a look that said, "You got yourself into this. You get yourself out."

"Well, it's not done yet." Parker wished he could sink below the table and suck his thumb the way he used to when he was very young and confronted by a situation that made him uncomfortable. "I don't really know if it's any good or not."

"I need to see it," Darby replied. "Man, I knew you had it in you!"

Parker glanced around again at the redhead at the other table.

This time she was looking straight at him.

Please don't come over here. . . .

"Yeah," he replied absentmindedly. "I'll show it to you later."

You stinking liar. Now you gotta write a song to get yourself out of this mess. And you can't write squat. You're getting pretty good at lying, you know that? You do a good job rationalizing your lies to Dax, so what's your reason this time?

Maybe Darby would forget.

As their attention shifted focus, Parker kicked Shanice in the leg to get her attention and ducked down again. "I'm serious, Shanice. How long have you known me?"

"I can tell you one thing," she whispered back. "I've been a Christian long enough to realize that we all get drug back in by our old temptations sometimes, Parker. That's all."

He sat back and folded his arms across his chest. "Not me, 'Nice. Like you said, that's old news. I have no old temptations that still have any hold on me."

"It's not always that easy, dawg," she replied, patting his arm. "Our old ways have a hard time letting go sometimes."

"No hold on me," he mumbled again, mostly to himself.

As the waitress returned with their food, he bowed his head, taking Shanice's and Jenna Rose's hands in his. They each hesitated, surely waiting for him to lead them in prayer as he usually did. Stealing a quick glance at the other table, he noticed the girl sitting across from Sierra eyeing him again.

Keep me focused, please, Lord.

Closing his eyes, he prayed over the food.

As soon as he muttered his "Amen," he dove into the platter of hot wings, not daring to look up at the girl from the next table. Shielding his eyes from her was as useless as hiding from the scream-scene in a cheesy horror movie. Her laugh echoed through the room, and again, he found himself stealing glances over his shoulder at her.

The girl said something and pointed. Parker's heart raced as he saw Sierra turn and face him. She smiled as he sunk lower into his seat.

Lord, please don't let this be a scene. I can't talk to her here. Not now. If You give me the chance another time, I will tell her all about You. Please.

Out of the corner of his eye, he saw her look at him a number of times. It was obvious to him she was trying to decide if she should come over and talk to him. He prayed again that she wouldn't.

He couldn't help but wonder where his sister was just then. Sierra and Corrina hardly did anything apart from one another. Even with his sister doing an internship at Dax's radio station, she usually had weekends free.

Maybe it was a good thing Corrina wasn't in the restaurant with Sierra. Like the rest of his family, she didn't know that Parker's best friends now were Churchies, or more importantly, that he had given himself to Jesus eight months before. Corrina knew he often went to a guy's house and hung out playing music. She knew he met up with other skaters—one of them being a biracial chick who dressed odd and often met him in front of the house. Together they skated all over town doing stupid tricks and occasionally busting up an arm or something. Corrina seemed pretty content to know he wasn't partying and getting into trouble—or at least not in the circles she was part of on the weekends—so she left him be.

Just like the rest of the family.

Eight months of skating or hitching a ride nine blocks to Faith Calvary Temple every Sunday morning at ten thirty and again on Sunday evening for the teen praise service and youth group meeting. Then there were a dozen paid local gigs with their band Second Rate. In all that time and all those events, not one person in the Blevins' household had ever once asked him where he was going.

It was just as well.

As he looked up from his empty plate of hot wings, Sierra and the others at her table were standing. Relief washed over him. He dropped his glance again, hoping to avoid eye contact if she turned around.

Just as he looked up again, she smiled at him. Watching her leave, a nagging thought crept into his belly. She hadn't revealed anything about the old Parker Blevins to his new friends. The new reputation he was trying to build for himself remained unscathed.

But was she going to reveal this new Parker Blevins to Corrina?

CHAPTER 7

T he van clock said 12:00 a.m. as it pulled up in front of Angelino's Pizzeria. Dax was still talking on the radio, but he had switched his attention over to a discussion with a call-in about eighties ballads. His other friends were quiet, leaving Parker to lament over their silence. Was it because of the deejay, that man they didn't know was his stepdad, or just the lateness of the hour that was causing the silence?

The house Elijah shared with his aunt and uncle sat close behind the pizza shop. The backyard had been turned into a storage area that connected the century-old home to the brick building many years before.

"Want some company?" Parker asked as Elijah stepped from the van.

"Sure," came the reply. Elijah's hand was still locked in Andria's. Swinging their arms playfully, he smiled and gave her a wink. "Meet me for a game in a bit?"

She returned the smile.

Parker shuffled his feet and tried to pretend he was perturbed at their exchange. Andria McKennitt looked so cute blushing through her Goth exterior. Her short hair was currently dyed such a deep black that it looked purple under most lights, and tonight it was spiked in all different directions. Covered in silver jewelry from her fingers to her ears, her heavy makeup contrasted strongly with her twin's style that required almost no makeup on her fair skin.

Barely a year ago, Parker was just another person in the school hall desperate to get out of her way as she passed. He and his friends would press themselves against the lockers and make rude comments. "Witch Girl" and "Freak" were just two of the names they called her. What a jerk he had been back then.

Never in a million years had he thought they would ever be friends. Even more unbelievable to him was the fact that she was a Bible-carrying, praying-at-the-pole type.

"You have work in the morning," she ventured in response to Elijah's question. "Probably shouldn't be on the computer playing games all night."

Elijah nodded in retrospect and dropped her hand. After a quick wave, he closed the door.

Parker stood beside his friend as the van pulled out of the parking lot. The rain had stopped, but the air still hung heavy with humidity. The bottom of Parker's pants soaked in a deep puddle, its warm wetness creeping up around his ankles.

The two boys had met just eight months ago, but their bond was like that of lifelong friends. In all the time Parker had known the quiet bass guitarist with a love for rock music, Elijah had been dating Andria. They really were the perfect rock 'n' roll couple—the tall, gaunt, moody guitarist who loved weird clothes together with the Goth chick who seemed to revel in the fact that people crossed to the other side of the mall to keep from possibly making eye contact. A regular Sid and Nancy. Kurt and Courtney.

Without the drugs and death and pain, of course.

But something seemed a bit odd beyond the way they looked when they were together.

"So, what next?" Elijah asked.

Parker shrugged. He loved the energy his bandmates and friends generated. He felt good, more alive somehow, when he was with them. Going home meant leaving that feeling behind. Things were different at home. Not bad different, but not like when he was on stage or in church with his friends. He hated the end of the day when he had to walk away from that. Everything seemed conditional at home. Affection was based on what you could do for each other instead of who you were. It was different with his friends. In Second Rate, Christ was among them, so their bond was about Him instead of them. In all of his life, he had never known anything like it, and he hated to leave it behind—even for just a few hours.

"Not tired," Parker mumbled as he tried to stifle a yawn.

With a kick, he sent a spray of small pebbles through the large puddle in the center of the lot. "Can I ask you a question?" Parker asked.

Elijah cocked his head to the side and nodded thoughtfully.

"I've never seen you kiss Andi." Maybe it was more of a comment than a question, but, either way, the subject had been on his mind. He hoped his friend saw the rest of it without him having to try to put it to words.

Drawing his tongue over his lip in thought, Elijah stared at his red Chuck Taylors for a moment.

Parker instantly regretted the statement and tried to take it back. "Dude, that was out of line."

"No, it wasn't," Elijah replied. "No big deal."

"Seriously, it was out of line. You don't have to say anything. It was stupid of me, and you don't have to say anything." Parker took a seat on the curb under the front awning of the empty pizza shop and started swirling a finger through the puddle in front of him. "I just realized that I've never seen you two kiss."

"That's because we haven't," Elijah answered simply. He seemed to be studying Parker's face for a reaction.

"No way. You're serious?"

Elijah sat down beside him. "Never once."

"But I thought you guys were a couple."

"I'm going to marry her," came the reply. "You might think it's weird that I already know that or whatever, but I do."

"No, that's cool." In all honesty, Parker was even more confused with this statement. If his friend knew this was the girl he wanted to marry, why wasn't he kissing her? There were other fifteen-year-olds out there using that same line of reasoning to explain some pretty intense relationship moves. Heck, Parker had probably used that line himself. Girls melted at statements like that. In fact, he was sure he'd used it more than once.

"Andi and I were in the same squad at a YMCA leaders thing a couple summers ago," Elijah explained. "We made abstinence pledges at the same time, and that year for Christmas we got each other promise rings." He held up his hand to show off the silver ring on his left ring finger. *Philippians 4:8* was carved around the band. "I don't even know when we became a couple exactly. It just sorta happened."

"But you've never even kissed her?"

He shook his head. "It just didn't seem right, you know? We kinda got into this relationship thanks to that pledge and those promise rings. We were supporting one another, praying for one another. It just seemed like we would be throwing that all away. When we realized how we felt, we decided to be faithful to that pledge—to God—first. Now it's almost a game. We went this far, and we both feel we can keep it going. Crazy, I know."

"Wow."

"Yeah, crazy." Elijah continued to play in the puddle in front of him, avoiding his friend's eye contact.

"Nah," Parker argued, "it's not crazy. It's really cool actually."

Elijah shrugged his shoulders. "I guess if I can keep this commitment, then I know I am capable of making a commitment for the rest of my life or something. And it shows me that she really loves me enough to keep that commitment to me as well. Probably a bit wack to someone like you, huh?"

"I. . .wow. . ." He stumbled for the right words, but none formed. So maybe his reputation had made its way into the Christian circles at school after all. And yet Elijah still wanted to hang out with him, despite knowing of his past.

Drawing in a deep breath, Parker continued to play in the puddle.

"You wanna crash at my house?" Elijah asked.

"I probably should go home."

"You sure? Aunt Cec always has a place for you. She's crazy about you."

Parker got to his feet. "You've got work in the morning. You need to get to bed. And I should get home so my mom doesn't freak."

Elijah looked at him again, concern and disbelief showing in his eyes. Parker knew that, like the others, Elijah wondered what was so bad about the Blevins' household that he never invited them over or spoke about his home life. He could only imagine what thoughts they must have had. Especially his friend here. Elijah was removed by child protective services from his drug-addict mom when he was only eight years old. After repeatedly being left home alone at night, Elijah had nearly burned the house down while trying to roast a marshmallow over a stove burner because he wanted a smore. He spent a few weeks in foster care and then eventually moved in with his mom's aunt and uncle. He'd lived with them ever since.

The thoughts that must go through his head.

Parker stood up and started across the parking lot as the humidity morphed into tiny raindrops. He didn't mind a bit. Walking in the rain was the perfect way to unwind after all the excitement he'd had.

And when he got home, he was going to check out that verse.

As Parker rounded the corner to his house, a soft glow greeted him through the glass block windows of the basement. Dameon often spent late nights in the rec room playing video games or shooting pool and nursing a beer or two, but Parker knew his brother was at work, so it wasn't him down there tonight.

He headed straight to the garage and found his board. At this time of night, if Corrina was in the basement, that meant she had friends over. If she was up past eleven without guests, she was in her room or on the computer or watching television upstairs. She wasn't one to care too much about pinball, pool, or the wide-screen TV.

Should have stayed with Elijah.

Right now he didn't need to deal with Sierra or any other friends of his sister. He also didn't feel like fielding the questions his sister would throw out when he headed for his room instead of joining them in the basement.

Stepping on the board, he coasted down the slight incline to the street. He'd just skate a bit and wait them out. His sister wanted to be known as a partier, but she loved her sleep too much to be up much past two in the morning. They would soon be heading upstairs. Then he would go in unnoticed and undisturbed.

The morning posed a new set of problems, but that could be dealt with, too. With everyone else in the house awake, his sister's guest would probably not try to hook up with him in any way. Questions he could work around. Staring down temptation in the guise of chestnut brown eyes when they were together alone in a cozy room was not something he wanted to attempt.

Because he was pretty sure that was a battle he was bound to lose.

The wheels purred against the asphalt as he picked up speed. There wasn't a car in sight and most of the houses were dark. The occasional sound of a dog or an engine across town broke up the silence. The air was still thick, but a few stars had begun to peek through the cloudy sky.

Swaying back and forth to keep his speed up, Parker ran his hand through his hair and stared straight ahead. Sleepiness crept over him. He turned back toward home, pumping his leg to gather speed, and continued past when he saw the lights downstairs still burning brightly.

Sleep would have to wait.

His thoughts went back to Dax. The man who was willing to buy him a guitar that cost more than most of his schoolmates' cars if he would only learn how to play an old hippie song. This was the man who fell in love with a heartbroken woman practically destroyed by a sudden divorce, and with her three kids as well. From the first day they had met him, Dax had never treated them like anything less than his own.

All of his friends' parents and families had been in the audience at least once, except for him. The sad thing was that Parker knew Dax would love Second Rate's sound. Parker could picture him up front at a gig with his arms crossed across his chest and his eyes beaming with pride as Parker ripped into a solo. He could see him bobbing his head to the beat with the precision of a music connoisseur. His nose would flare, and he would fight back a smile as he realized how good they sounded. He would stand his ground, unmoving, as the crowd around him bounced and crowded in with each new song.

"Churches are worse than thieves," Parker remembered his stepfather saying to him once as they passed three teens carrying signs offering a car wash. "Thieves at least just take your money and run, but churches prey on weak people who desperately want to believe that there is something out there higher than them in control of things."

"But isn't there something higher out there than us?" Parker had asked. He had always thought there was. God was something—even if he didn't really know what.

" 'God' is the creation of man, Parker. We are not the ones who were 'created.' This country was founded on the principles that religion is a man's choice, and the right to say 'no' to that choice is not to be taken lightly. You are not one of those weak people, Parker. You're a leader, not a follower, and you don't need a higher power telling you how to live your life."

As they sat at the stoplight, Parker had watched the group behind the building working on a car. "The sign says they're raising money to fund a mission trip to deliver food to the poor in Mexico," Parker had commented. "That doesn't sound so bad."

"Just an excuse to control the way other people are living. Like I said, they are preying on the weak."

"Can we give them some money at least to help out? I mean, feeding the poor is a good thing, right?"

Dax had laughed as the light changed. "I wonder how much of their money raised is really going to go to those children and how much is going into their travel costs, food bills, and hotel stays on their way to their mission trip? Scam, that's all it is. Indoctrination of their youth disguised as charity work and nothing else. There are plenty of chances to help the needy without the hidden Christian agenda, Parker. We'll find another way to put our money to real use, okay?"

Parker had been eight or nine at the time—it was soon after the wedding. He had strained to see those kids working so hard to make it look like they were making money for people they didn't know, and he wondered what they were going to do with it after they were through. What kind of parents did they have to allow them to tell lies and steal money like that?

Dax talked about religion a lot after he moved in. Over dinner, he would rant about the number of public school systems across the country that still taught religion classes and how public leaders would hold prayer time before their meetings. He would complain about prayer groups being held on school grounds after hours and the references to God printed on money.

Activism was what he preached—standing up for what we believe and our right to believe it. "We don't need someone else to tell us what's right or moral."

One day as he dropped Parker off at school, Dax took him by the shoulders and told him that it was his "patriotic duty to refuse to say the Pledge of Allegiance before class" and that he expected him to sit in protest of its religious overtones.

When Parker asked him why, he responded, "You gotta fight the good fight, Parker. We don't believe in God. We believe in the Constitution, and it's our constitutional duty to stand up against those who try to impose their version of morality on us. You're a leader, remember? A leader has to take a stand sometimes."

Parker had nodded, sure of only one word that Dax had said—*duty*. It was his duty to not stand for the pledge. His daddy had faded into occasional phone call oblivion by then, and that third grader was willing to follow any *duty* Dax Blevins said he was called to do. As long as Dax was interested in his family, Parker was willing to be interested in anything he was told to do.

He walked into his classroom and sat down at his desk, but as every minute ticked off the clock, fear was building in his stomach. The teacher called for them to stand up. Everyone came to their feet beside their desks, except for the mop-headed boy in the middle row. "Parker Blevins," the teacher said, "it's time for the Pledge." They stared at each other in wait. Her eyes seemed to stare right through him as she waited for him to follow her directions. Disobedient little boys who didn't believe in God and stayed in their chairs all in the name of "constitutional duty" during the Pledge were trouble. Parker was sure they must be banished to a basement hole during the best parts of the school day. Dax or no Dax, he couldn't give up his recess. Duty or no duty, he got to his feet and said the Pledge with the rest of the class.

When Dax picked him up from school and asked if he sat out the Pledge, Parker had nodded and pretended to be really interested in his science book. "Did you get in trouble? Because they aren't allowed to punish you for that." This time the boy shook his head no. For the rest of that night, Dax wore the biggest smile, and that brought a matching grin to Parker's face. And Parker still remembered how good it had felt to please Dax, even with having to lie in the process. That day he had done more than his *duty;* he had made his stepdad proud.

You've been lying to him for a long time, Parker admitted to himself. Mindlessly, he continued to push his skateboard with one foot.

He had his reasons. Even if he wasn't completely sure what they were anymore.

CHAPTER 9

Parker came to a stop and stepped off his board. Every muscle in his body ached under the weight of the early hour. Looking up at the two-story home with the rickety white and green front porch in front of him, he wondered how he had gotten there. He thought he was skating indiscriminately, merely passing time until his sister shuffled off to bed. But his body had brought him here.

The soft, bouncing glow of television light played through the living room windows. No other lights in the house were on.

She was still up.

Glancing at his arm, he shook his head and stifled a yawn. That wrist hadn't seen a watch in months, yet he still found himself turning to it for help when he needed it. Watch or not, the time was late, and he found it a bit surprising that she was still awake.

You went this far. You have to talk to her now.

But what if she wasn't home alone?

The question quickly faded out of importance. If she had any friends staying over, they were sure to not be the type to hit on him. Other than the twins, Shanice, or Amber, who else would be there?

Reverend Brinley was most likely not the form lying on the sofa watching videos.

The creaky porch was sure to scare her—possibly even wake up her father—if he tried to trudge across it. Neither was an acceptable possibility.

Maybe he should just go home. Then he heard a noise from the side window that overlooked the driveway. He hurried over to the glass and peered inside.

"Hey," he whispered through the screen. "Jenna, you up?"

The television went mute.

"Jenna."

Running his fingers through his hair, he strained to look into the room to see if there was any indication of her hearing him. He didn't want to wake her if she was asleep.

"Man, Parker," her voice sounded before she appeared through the darkened room. "You scared the snot out of me. What are you doing?"

"Skating," he replied before he realized how silly it sounded.

"It's almost three in the morning!"

"Man, it's that late?" he backed away and kicked his board up into his hand. "I'm sorry. I didn't realize it was that late. I shouldn't have woke you up."

She disappeared from the window.

Parker glanced around him, unsure of what to do.

Just as he was considering heading home and apologizing in the morning, the front door opened, and Jenna Rose stepped out. Her blond hair was pulled back off her face with a pink bandana similar to those Shanice often wore. *But 'Nice would never wear pink,* he thought. Jenna Rose wore baggy gray pajama pants and a belly-button-baring T-shirt with "g'night" emblazoned in pink across it.

"I had to put a shirt on," she stated.

Parker squeezed his eyes shut again, trying to keep an image from forming in his mind.

"I was in my robe," she added, grinning at his reaction. "What are you doing out so late?"

"Why are you still up?" he asked. "I really shouldn't have come over like this. It's way too late, and I wasn't thinking."

After grumbling about the wet sidewalk, she climbed down the stairs and stood facing him in the driveway. "Parker, what are you doing at my house in the middle of the night if you weren't expecting me to be up?"

A half-dozen answers flew through his head so fast that for a second he couldn't grab onto any single one of them. "I'm stalking you," he finally replied, flashing a smile.

She shuffled her feet slightly, crossed her arms, and grinned confidently. Parker called that move her "pretending-to-be-embarrassed dance." Once upon a time, he would have fallen for it, but not anymore. "Well, thanks for telling me. You need to work on that. I don't think stalkers are usually so open about it."

"I guess I'm not your run-of-the-mill stalker."

"Guess not," she replied. "Everything okay?"

He nodded and held his skateboard up. "I was just out skating, and I ended up in the area. When I saw your light on, I had to say hi. So, hi."

"You just happened to be in my neighborhood?" She smirked, tilting her head to the side. "In the middle of the night, of all the places in this big city you could skate to, you just happened to come into my neighborhood?"

"What's so weird about that? I needed to clear my head a bit. I started skating. This is where I ended up. I didn't question it."

"Hmm." Jenna Rose took the board from him and dropped it to the ground. "Maybe you ended up here for a reason," she said boldly, holding his gaze for a few seconds. Then she dropped her attention to the skateboard at their feet. "Anyway, what's so exciting about this thing that it would bring you out at three in the morning when it's all wet and muggy?" She tentatively placed one foot on the board and rolled it from side to side.

"Jump on and find out," Parker urged. He took her hand and coaxed both her feet onto the deck. She wobbled, giggling, as he guided her across the driveway. "Bend your knees a bit," he instructed. "Balance."

"I *am* balancing!" She grabbed his shoulder with both hands.

Laughing, he pushed her far arm away. "You can't balance if you have a death grip on me. Just relax! You're doing fine," he tried to reassure her. "Spread your feet out a little bit more, and keep your knees bent."

"You never look like that when you're on this thing," she pointed at her soft shadow cast from the streetlamp above. Her shadow looked more like that of a soccer goalie or a swamp monster with its arms out-stretched and the stance of her wide, bent knees.

"When you can stand on a board by yourself and go down this drive-way," Parker replied, "then you can talk to me about the way I skate, okay?" He placed his hands high on her hips and walked her to the other side of the drive.

They continued to cross the driveway at a snail's pace. Jenna Rose would protest each time he tried to remove his hands, but the truth was, he didn't want to move his hands. He just wanted to touch her, to feel her breathe and laugh, and watch her try to do something just because he liked to do it. The need for sleep was gone. If they were together, he didn't need to rest.

"Think you can do it yourself yet?"

"No!" she giggled, cupping her hands over his. "Don't you let go of me."

It took every ounce he could muster to move her hands from his. Adjusting her upper body to balance better, he shook his head. "Okay, now balance."

With a little nudge, he released her, and the board rolled slowly back across the driveway. With arms outstretched like someone pretending to surf, she wobbled her way into the grass and jumped off the board. "I did it. I did it," she sang, dancing a silly victory dance.

Parker walked across the drive, put his feet on the board, and jumped straight up. The board twisted in the air under his suspended feet and then landed back on its wheels with Parker on top of it.

"Show-off," she snipped, pretending to pout. She turned her back to him and crossed her arms, but not before a smile crept across her face.

"That was an ollie. With enough lessons, you can learn to do that," he promised and scooped up the board, bumping her elbow lightly in the process. "Not bad for a first lesson."

I'll give you a million more if you want them.

"Who said I was interested in learning to ride this thing?" Pulling the board from his grasp, she held it out to survey its surface more closely. A comedic skeletal figure danced across a large black patch between the wheel decks. Most of the figure's blue paint had been chipped away. A sticker with a strange-looking cross emblem and the word "Independent" scrawled through it covered the rest of the black spot.

"That's an Eric Nash board," he explained proudly. "It's a sweet ride. Bit of road rash there, but it's still going after three years now. Of course, I've gone through some wheels in that time and trucks, too, but that's alright. I got a new Birdhouse Santos Robot deck last year for Christmas, but why trash on a new board when you've got a perfectly good one? Birdhouse boards are sweet. That's Tony Hawk's company, you know? But this Nash is like a vintage board."

He brought his glance up from the skateboard just in time to watch her move closer. Then her lips were on his. An explosion of senses streamed through his body. Frozen, he let the board drop and closed his eyes. Her lips were so soft. The kiss was innocent but lingering, like she was waiting for him to react.

But he couldn't react.

Pulling away would add to the awkwardness that was bound to follow, and Parker didn't want to compound it. Jenna Rose was his friend and his bandmate, and he couldn't let anything get in the way of that.

Kissing her back—as much as he wanted to—would be an even worse option.

He didn't want to pull away. He wanted to kiss her back. He wanted to express all the emotions he had bottled up inside since that first day he had walked into her empty house with a box in hand. Kissing her had been on his mind the first time he saw her.

Slowly, she pulled away, her eyes still closed.

Parker studied her face intently, looking for some sign of what lay ahead between them.

Something like shards of glass seemed to roll around in his stomach as he tried to come up with the right words to say. "Wh—why'd you do that?" he stammered.

"Because I had no idea what you were talking about," she replied. Her eyes studied his intently.

"You could have told me to stop talking," he replied, his head swirling.

"I thought I did. I just did it in my own way."

Pointing toward the road, Parker stepped back on the board. Her eyes were searching his very being, and he needed to get home before she saw into his heart. She didn't need to know what lay there. "I should go," he whispered. "You need to get to bed, and I. . .I need to go."

With her hands behind her back, she leaned forward and kissed him again, much quicker this time—like a peck one would give a child. Her face glowed as she bit her lip softly and looked at him. "Okay," she said uncertainly.

Before he could change his mind, he leaned down and kissed her.

CHAPPTER 110

Parker crawled into his bed fully clothed and tucked himself into a ball under his comforter. Pulling his pillow over his head, he tried to get comfortable. His body was spent, exhausted from him pushing it past its already worn-out state from the evening before.

You never should have gone skating.

He knew he had no business being out that late at night, and he really had no business being at Jenna Rose's house. Thrashing his head against the mattress, he sighed loudly. This had to have been one of the stupidest stunts he ever pulled.

Even though his body was begging for sleep, he simply couldn't settle down to rest. Jumping up from bed, he stormed into the bathroom. He turned the faucet on and let his cupped hands fill with water.

"Why do you have to be so stupid?" he asked his reflection in the mirror. "You probably just ruined the whole band." He splashed the water in his face. "Was that worth it? It was just a stupid little kiss."

Studying himself, he sighed and ran a hand through his hair. The girls always loved his curly locks. He didn't particularly like them himself. It took considerable time to take care of his hair. It had to be washed every day, and figuring out the right amount of hair products to keep him from looking like some frizzy clown head was hit-and-miss each day. He could deal with the occasional jock-crack about his 'do—the way the girls were into his style always more than made up for it.

Most of those shaved-head football players just seemed jealous anyway. No, he didn't like his hair at all really. It was a vanity thing. His hair looked good, that was all. The extra work was worth the attention.

"Maybe it'd be easier to deal with the girl situation if you weren't trying so hard to get their attention," he told his reflection.

With new resolve, he threw open the bathroom cupboard and found the pair of haircutting scissors his mom kept there. Dameon's clippers were another option, but he resisted and closed the door. He didn't have the guts to go as far as Elijah's look.

Biting his lip, he pulled a curl out straight and opened the scissors. His eyes fell closed as he allowed the scissors to snap shut. The hair fell in a spiral into the sink. "That wasn't too bad," he murmured, examining the chunk of bangs that barely fell below his hairline.

Again and again, he chopped chunks of hair from the top of his head, allowing the scissors to move indiscriminately across his curls. More and more spirals fell in clumps into the basin.

You look like a freak. You should have at least gone and had it done professionally.

"Still would have looked too good," he mumbled, running his fingers through the mass of hair left on his head.

Shaking his head above the sink to allow any stragglers to fall, he laughed at the sight of his new 'do.

They are all going to so freak tomorrow.

Returning to his room after disposing of the evidence, he crawled back into bed and tried to get his mind off the kiss. *God, why did You let me do such a thing?*

Tossing and turning, he ended up resting on his back and still staring into the darkness. No matter how exhausted he was, there would be no sleep for him tonight, he was sure of it. Images and emotions mixed in with his thoughts as he reached for his headphones on the nightstand.

Music soothes the savage beast, right? Well, maybe it can calm me down and get me back on track. Stupid, stupid, stupid.

He placed the portable CD player on his stomach and fitted the headphones over his ears, sighing again. What was going to happen tomorrow when he had to face her again? What was he going to say when she came at him wanting to know what their next step was going to be?

Temptation. . .

It was a word that had never had a place in his vocabulary before finding Christ. If it did, it was as a joke. Dax termed it "Christianese—another word created by *them* to control the rest of us."

Funny how it now held a central spot in his mind.

God brought Jenna Rose into their lives so they could fulfill a purpose. He was sure of it. He knew that the very first Sunday morning when he had first heard her sing. Her being there—her friendship—was supposed to be a blessing.

So why was her presence also a temptation?

"You shouldn't have kissed her, you stupid," he said aloud.

She did it first.

He tried to shake away that defiant little voice from the back of his mind. For months he had done well to stifle the voice of his flesh that still cried out during his weakest moments.

What's the harm in having a girlfriend? She's a Christian.

He closed his eyes again at the way the last sentence flowed through his thoughts. It sounded like the girls in the alleyway. It mocked him. It sounded like the old him—the Parker who believed everything Dax had fed him about the "Christian hypocrite."

Placing the headphones over his ears, he pressed PLAY. Jenna Rose's voice filled his ears. Bolting up, he grabbed the CD player and pulled the CD from the machine. The sweet sound of her melody was not what he needed to hear right now. Fumbling in the darkness, he found another CD on his end table and put it in.

"Lately I've been wandering off the narrow path. . . ."

Settling back into his thick pillow, he crossed his hands behind his head. Parker stared at the ceiling, amazed at the vehicles God used to reach out to him. Music was definitely one of those connections. He felt the tension subside in his body. How had he gone fifteen years of his life thinking that everything happened by chance, from the phone call from a friend at the right time to the perfect song playing over the airwaves and calming his nerves? How could he ever have thought that was all luck?

"And I hate the way I feel inside," he sang softly into the darkness with the song filling his head. "And I know I need You in my life."

With his eyes now growing heavy, he settled into his pillow and sighed one last time.

"And I promise to make the sacrifice. . ." were the last words Parker heard before he drifted off to sleep.

CCHHAAPPTTEERR 111

Sacrifice...The taste of the word still lay thick in his mouth as he woke from sleep.

Bright morning sunlight poured through the seams of his blinds, making him pull his blanket over his head. Usually he made sure his blinds were closed before crawling into bed and playing a PlayStation game or two. That was his normal nightly ritual.

What was he supposed to be sacrificing? He was so certain before meeting Jenna Rose that for him, sacrifice meant no dating. What else did he have that would be worth sacrificing? What else could he do to show this Savior that Parker Blevins meant business when he said, "I give my life to You, Lord"? Before becoming a Christian, he had poured all of himself into the pursuit of the opposite gender. Everything about Parker Blevins used to be about getting the girls, but when he came to Christ, that changed. For the past eight months, his life was about getting to know Christ. And now he just wasn't sure how to proceed.

Could he have Christ and a girlfriend, too?

Fumbling for his alarm clock that was now lost in the folds of his bedding, he grimaced at the stiffness of his joints. Whatever the hour, his body had not had a proper amount of time to rejuvenate itself.

"One of these days you're going to choke yourself in your sleep with those headphones," his mother commented from the doorway with a basket of clothes tucked in her arms. "You were in here singing loud enough last night that I don't know why you bother even wearing those things. Definitely not for our benefit." She plopped the basket down in the center of his bed, just missing his scurrying limbs as they got out of her way. "What did you do to your hair?"

"Sorry," he mumbled, rubbing his face. He sat up and located the alarm clock's cord peaking from under his pillow. "I just wanted something different."

"Hungover or not, it's time to get up," she replied with a knowing smile. "Well, it is different."

"I'm not hungover," he defended, rolling his eyes.

"Sure," she said, swatting at his feet as she made her way to the open door. "Just like your sister's not either. Go look at yourself in the mirror, and maybe then you'll think twice about drinking." She shook her head. "All those beautiful curls."

"I didn't do it because I was drinking, Mom."

"I want this room clean today before you go anywhere. Understand?"

"I'm not hungover!" he yelled at the closing door. "I was just out late last night."

It was senseless to argue with her, he knew that. When his mom had her mind made up about something, no one could persuade her otherwise. Her three kids were rock 'n' rollers so therefore they must all be partying every weekend as well. End of story. As long as he and his siblings weren't doing their partying while getting behind the wheel of a car, his parents didn't seem to care. "Responsibility" was another big word in their vocabulary.

"Like anyone cares," his sister called out as she passed outside his room.

Stuffing a hand under his mattress, Parker retrieved his Bible and thought again about the engraving on Elijah's ring. It was rather ironic actually. Other kids hid bad magazines under their bed, but for Parker, it was the safest place to put his Bible.

He scoured his mind, trying to recall the verse on his friend's ring, but it wouldn't come to mind. "Philippians," he said aloud. "Philippians what?" Whatever it was, it had something to do with abstinence. That's what Elijah said the whole "promise" thing was about. Parker decided to skim through the whole book until he found the right verse.

"Waiting until marriage for what?" Parker mumbled. The sex part he could understand. He'd heard enough in his eight months as a Christian to know what God expected about that, but was there a ban on kissing, too?

His heart sank at the thought of it. Surely he hadn't done anything *that* wrong last night with the kiss. "Finally, brothers, whatever is true, whatever is noble, whatever is right, whatever is pure, whatever is lovely, whatever is admirable—" Parker stopped and flipped a couple of pages ahead. Was this what the ring had written on it? He turned back and continued reading, this time aloud, "If anything is excellent or praiseworthy—think about such things."

"What's that?"

He looked up to see his sister standing in the doorway. In his concentration, he hadn't heard the door open. Corrina sneered as she looked at the book with her hands on her hips. By the grin, Parker could tell that she knew exactly what he had in his hands.

"It's a Bible," he said, surprised at the conviction in his own voice. For someone who had dreaded this moment for almost a year, he was amazed.

She closed the door behind her and sat down on the edge of his bed. "Did you steal it from a hotel or something?"

"No," he retorted. Deep down he wasn't sure if he was more disgusted at the obvious way his family viewed him—everything from hangovers to hotel thefts—or the fact that he hadn't worked hard to dispel such thoughts from their minds. Did his own family really know that little about him?

"Where'd it come from?" She flopped back on his high captain's bed and swung her bare feet lazily. Her hair, with the same curly consistency as her brother's, fell in a damp wreath around her head. She reached out for the book, but he held fast.

"It's mine."

"What are you doing with a Bible?" She snatched it from him and sat up.

"I'm reading it. Now give it back." He struggled to free himself from the blankets holding him fast.

"Where'd you get it?"

"I bought it," he replied, grabbing for his most precious possession. She turned her back toward him and flipped through the pages. She might as well have been looking into his soul and laughing by reading those pages he had highlighted and wrote private notes to himself in the margins.

"No way!" she laughed. "Why are you reading it?" A bulletin from last week's church service fell out in her lap. "What's this?"

"Give it to me," he said, reaching for the paper.

She held tight. "You go to church?" She emphasized each word with a pause between them.

"I said give me that," he barked, pulling himself free from the blankets.

"Are you serious? You go to church? It's for a girl, right? You've got the hots for some Churchie girl, don't you?" Corrina fell backward on the bed, holding her stomach in laughter. "I can't believe it," she howled. "Dax's golden boy is a Bible-beater."

"Man, Cori," he mumbled, shoving at her with his foot. "You don't have to make it sound so stupid."

"Just wait 'til Dax finds out about this. So, what? You messin' with her and decided you'd make it all better by going to church with her or something?" She sat up and pointed a finger at him. "Repent and ye shall be saved!"

Parker bolted up. "Don't you tell him anything! I will tell him when I'm ready." He ran his fingers through his hair, momentarily shocked by the lack of curls. "And I'm not messin' with anyone. It doesn't have anything to do with a girl."

She stopped laughing and looked at him. "What's it worth to you?"

"You know he'll flip, Cori," Parker pleaded. "Don't tell him. Please let me be the one to do it."

Corrina paused for a few moments. "Church, huh?"

"Church is really cool."

"I'm sure it is," she giggled again. She stood up, dropping the book beside him on the bed. "You just watch yourself, Parker I could pop at any time." She turned the doorknob with one hand and brushed her hair out of her eyes with the other as she looked over her shoulder at him. "And don't kid yourself, Parker," she added, her tone the most serious she had voiced all morning. "Everything with you is always about a girl."

CHAPTER 12

Parker stuffed the Bible back under the mattress and headed for his dresser. On the way, he stripped down to his boxers and flipped the radio on. Grabbing a pair of khaki shorts with large pockets, boxers, a white T-shirt, and a blue polo shirt, he headed for the bathroom across the hall.

Once upon a time, his room was his haven. It was small by some standards but perfect for him. His captain's bed had plenty of drawers underneath and sat much higher than most beds. He had an additional dresser—because he had no closet—a desk, and a nightstand as well. The large beanbag took up most of his floor. One corner held his collection of boards—his new one, a long board, and two old ones that he kept for sentimental reasons. He also kept his snowboard and a pair of in-line skates there. Posters of emo and other punk bands covered the wall and a Vans T-shirt signed by Tony Hawk and two other pro skaters was tacked up above his television.

Lately he tried to be out of the house as much as possible. Even his own bedroom seemed like enemy territory.

The bathroom door was closed. With a sigh, he pounded open-handed on the door, letting his clothes fall to the floor. Corrina's room led into the bathroom, and she often forgot to unlock the door. "Cori," he called out, "you left the door locked. Come on, Cori. Open the door!"

The door swung open.

As he reached down to pick up the clothes he had dropped, he caught sight of a figure wrapped in a towel crossing the bathroom to his sister's room. Even with a towel encircling her head, he knew it had to be Sierra. She left the door open and stayed in his line of vision.

He dropped his eyes and walked through the misty room. Then he pulled the door to his sister's room shut behind her. He locked it as well.

Temptations. . .sacrifice. Time to find out if what they say about cold showers being therapeutic is true.

He spun the cold water spigot on so the water shot out full blast.

When he was done with his shower, he dressed quickly and turned his attention toward his new hairstyle. With a healthy dollop of gel, he gooped his hair up and worked the product in, letting his newly shorn curls stick up, fall, and crisscross in whatever direction each piece wanted to go. The crazy spiked mess hid the various lengths well.

As he turned the corner to get his shoes out of his room, he noticed the door was now open.

"Man, Dameon!" Parker yelled, his temper flaring. "Get your dog out of my room!"

As he swung around to stomp into the living room, the shiny black Rottweiler lifted his head and stared at Parker from the sunny spot in the middle of the living room floor. Ozzy was still a pup, despite his full-grown body, and, with Dameon working most nights, he tried to slip into Parker's room as often as possible. The last thing Parker wanted was to share his cramped quarters with a two-hundred-pound dog.

"My dog's in here, doof," came the reply. "Watch it, or I'll sic him on you."

"That dog's too stupid to find his own food bowl most of the time," Parker said shortly while keeping one eye on the canine. Ozzy gave a big sigh and laid his head back down on his paws.

Parker turned his attention back to the mystery at hand.

What happened to my music? And who's in my room?

The radio was left playing at barely a whisper of a decibel. Parker knew it was unlikely in this house that anyone was offended by the volume and had turned it down. Actually, it was quite common to hear a hodgepodge collection of rock sounds coming from various rooms in their house. He entered, eyeing the open door suspiciously, and was immediately relieved that he had gotten dressed in the bathroom instead of rushing across the hall in a towel like he normally did.

Sierra, already wearing too much makeup and a tight, short skirt, was in his beanbag chair, a PlayStation controller in hand. She craned her neck to see him as he walked in the room and flashed him a wide smile.

Lord, why are You doing this to me?

"Since when did we become so shy?" she asked sweetly.

"What are you doing in my room?" Parker stood in the doorway, flashing dirty looks at Corrina down the hallway. She looked back and smiled wickedly. With a shooing movement of the hands, she scurried out of sight. So this was all a plan worked out between the two girls to give him some time alone with Sierra.

Once upon a time he would have been grateful.

"It's been forever since we've played PlayStation," she pouted. "I was just missing it. Seeing you last night reminded me that I was just missing you. Omigosh, what'd you do to your hair?"

Parker glared at his sister again down the hall of the ranch home. From the living room, Corrina was watching him as well. This time she motioned for him to go in his room. "Did you just come over here last night to see me?" he asked, turning his attention back to the girl in his beanbag. " 'Cuz that's a really shady thing to do to my sister."

"As if, Parker," she laughed. "Like Cori cares."

His sister crossed her arms, letting her nostrils flare in disbelief at Parker's insinuation.

Feeling trapped, Parker walked into his bedroom and stood in front of his dresser. He wasn't trying his sister; he knew she could decide to tell Dax his news any time she wanted. But when Dax did find out, Parker wanted to make sure it was on his terms and not anyone else's. The longer he let Corrina think she held something over his head, the more bored she'd get with it and just eventually give up. Such was the essence of their sibling relationship.

"Sit down with me and play PlayStation," she urged, indicating the space on the floor in front of her. The old Parker often sat on the floor between her knees as they played games. He would tickle under her knee or try to grab her controller to throw her off base. After a while, she'd get bored and mess with his hair while he played. She used to always talk about braiding his hair into cornrows, but she'd get bored with that after a row or two. Parker knew it was just an excuse for her to get close to him, but he never minded.

He took the controller but leaned on the edge of the bed instead.

"You've been really busy this summer, haven't you? You're like never home when I'm here," she said, crossing her feet in front of her and settling back into the oversized bag. "Whatcha been up to?"

"Stuff," he replied, feeling very much like a little kid being grilled by his parents when all he wanted to do was get outside. But he was trapped. His mom had told him he wasn't allowed to go anywhere if he didn't clean his room up first, and, to mom, that meant beds stripped and remade, clothes sorted in the laundry room, floor clean and swept, and all shelves and furniture tops neat.

He looked about his room. It would probably take him all of fifteen minutes to straighten it up. There were a few papers littered across his desk, some dirty clothes on the floor, a basket of clothes to be put away on his bed, and a couple of soda cans resting beside his laptop. It would just take a few minutes if he didn't have an unexpected guest.

Asking Sierra to help was out of the question. He'd been around her enough to know that she probably didn't have any chores of her own to do, and she definitely was allergic to helping others do theirs. He'd seen her sitting at the table looking thoroughly bored as Corrina washed dishes many times.

Jenna Rose would probably help clean them.

"Which one was your girlfriend?" she asked, not looking up from the game.

"Huh?" he grunted.

"Last night at the restaurant. Which one was your girlfriend?"

If only he could be like Tony Hawk in the game and just dive out the window and land on a waiting board to get away from all this. "I don't have a girlfriend," he replied. "Those are all just friends of mine."

"I just figured there had to be a girlfriend since I never see you anymore," she commented. Her voice sounded sad. "And there were plenty of girls with you last night. I just figured one of them must have gotten a hold on you."

"They're. . ." He stopped himself from finishing the sentence. If he told her about the band, chances were good that she would want to come check them out, and that would not be a good thing. And if she came to check them out, chances were even better that his sister would come as well, and that would be even worse. Corrina would love their sound, and when she found a band that she loved, she never shut up about it. No, neither Sierra nor Corrina could know about Second Rate. At least not until he figured out how he was going to tell Dax about his newfound beliefs.

His conscience lectured him immediately: *You should tell her the truth. You should tell her about Christ and that you are sorry about the way you used her before and that it can't continue anymore. You should tell her now before she makes a move on you and puts you in an awkward position, because do you really think you are strong enough to resist?*

But the words just jumbled around in his mouth, unsure of the order in which to come. He could talk about his faith to a roomful of strangers, but he got tongue-tied at the idea of talking to the one person he had probably hurt the most in his lifetime.

"Nah," was all that came out.

"So there's still hope for me?" she asked playfully. Parker detected more than playfulness in her voice. He was now more than just the kid brother of her friend, more than someone to mess around with on the weekends when she had nothing better to do. Parker Blevins was on the verge of manhood. He was a handsome, good-natured teen groomed by a rock 'n' roll family for the road to stardom. The cynical little voice in the back of his mind was sure that her interests in him were less than sincere—perhaps she was looking to grab hold of his heart now and ride on his coattails.

"Watch out for that truck!" he chirped, thankful that the game gave him a distraction from answering her question. "It's my turn."

Leaning over, she started pushing buttons on his controller.

"You cheat! Quit it." He laughed, swatting at her hands.

"Well, that's more like the Parker I know," she replied, pinching his calf. "Make that one stay. Stuffy, boring guy that was just here, you go away."

Just ignore her.

Corrina's head popped into the doorway. "Am I interrupting anything important?" she queried.

Sierra settled back into the chair and turned her attention back to the game. "Not yet," she replied mockingly.

Standing up, Parker let the controller topple to the fuzzy blue carpet. "I've got to chase both of you out," he said authoritatively. "I've got stuff to do today, and mom says I have to clean my room first."

"Let mom do it," Corrina replied. "She might be interested in what she finds."

With one hand, Parker grabbed for Sierra's hand and with the other he pushed his sister from the room. "Out," he commanded, tired of this game the girls were playing. Sierra was not so easy to budge. With a jerk of the arm, she pulled him down on top of her as Corrina shut the door.

Parker scrambled to his knees and backed away from her almost as soon as he lost his balance.

Frowning, she wrinkled her mouth and shook her head, a laugh escaping despite her apparent angst. "You act like I'm going to bite you or something. What's your problem?"

Talk to her about the change in you. Apologize for the hurt you've caused her, and tell her the truth about who you are now. Why is it so hard for you to admit this change?

His conscience wouldn't let up, but Parker shoved the thoughts deeper. "I have to clean my room," he said again, pointing to the door.

"I think you should go now."

"Maybe I think you don't really want me to," she said stubbornly, holding fast in her chair.

You're right. I don't want you to go anywhere. The voice of his flesh was trying to push out of the back of his mind again, trying to take control at the moment Parker had feared most—when he was alone and staring into those chestnut-colored eyes.

He shoved the voice back. "No, Sierra. I really do. I'm sorry about everything because, you know, things never should have happened between us, and I regret that they did."

Her voice wavered between sadness and sharp anger as she jumped to her feet. "You regret it? Well, thank you very much for the happy memories!"

Parker ran his hand through his hair and thumped his head against the side of his dresser. She was too angry to talk with right now. Here it was his first real opportunity to share the gospel with someone close to him, and he had blown it. He meant exactly what he had said—he did regret their previous actions together because what happened wasn't the way things were supposed to happen for Christians, but he felt terrible that his words stung. Her eyes were burning through him, firmly fixed on his soul. She was waiting for him to cave like he had done in the past. Former girlfriends and all the intentions of faithfulness to those relationships had not slowed his attraction to her in the past. She still thought this was all about another girl.

BC—before Christ came into my life.

Like father, like son.

His father's love for women and lack of control over that obsession had killed his marriage, his relationship with his children, and his connection with his parents. It had consumed him until it was all he had left. Parker sat up straight and shook his head. It was done. He was not going to be like his father anymore.

She brushed the wrinkles from her short skirt and pointed back at him. "You just remember what you turned down, Parker Blevins, when your little girlfriend isn't all you think she is."

Parker got to his feet and walked to the door. He held it open and nodded in response.

Of course she thinks it's about a girl. With me it's always about a girl, right?

"I'll see you around, Sierra," he said. He opened the door leading into the hallway, hoping she would see the finality in the gesture and leave him alone.

CHAPTER 13

Less than a half an hour later, Parker emerged from his clean bedroom and headed to the kitchen for something to eat. His stomach grumbled as it was well past the hungry stage. He knew he was never going to wake up if he didn't get something in his belly. It had been a long time since he'd slept that far past noon. Darby was sure to be freaking right now and wondering where he was.

Dragging a hand along the wall as he passed through the hallway, Parker glanced at the lines of framed pictures from their childhood. Photos of vacations were littered among backyard snapshots and school portraits. Not so much as a thought of Daniel Chapman in any of them.

Their house was the final reminder of his birth father Parker allowed himself to keep. His dad had gladly given over the house to Parker's mom in exchange for his freedom. The house, the kids, and the Volvo station wagon were all hers as long as he got to say good-bye.

Sometimes, when he walked down the narrow hallway from the living room, Parker thought he could hear his dad down in the basement in his workshop. He would come home from work and disappear down there, always starting projects and never finishing them. For his dad, the workshop had been a good place to hide from the real world and play make-believe in the one he had created in his head.

After Dax married his mom, they decided to turn the workshop that had been strictly Parker's dad's space into a family rec room.

Dozens of partially finished tables, chairs, and chests were carried out of the basement. Mom was bent on pitching them, but Dax wanted to donate them to a local workshop for the mentally handicapped. It was good wood, he pointed out, and they could finish those projects or recycle them somehow. Mom was pleased with the humanitarian end of the suggestion, and all three of her kids put the *new* man in the house on a pedestal for making their mom so happy.

She called her ex-husband, now in Michigan, and asked if he wanted her to box up his tools and woodworking books and send them to him. "Nope," he had replied. Seems he and the new wife had built a huge house outside of Lansing, complete with a heated three-car garage and a much larger workshop. As a final jab, he had suggested that her new husband could use them and consider the tools a wedding gift from him.

Mom had carted five thousand dollars worth of woodshop tools off to the mentally handicapped workshop as well. But that was only after Dax spent two hours talking her out of just breaking them all and mailing the pieces off to Lansing instead.

If not for the rec room downstairs, the ranch-style house would be much too small for their family. But thanks to the divorce, his mom owned the house free and clear. She said there was no reason for them to go into debt for a bigger house when Parker, Corrina, and Dameon were almost grown. With no house payment to take out of her salary, they would make it on her earnings.

Of course, at that time, she wasn't expecting her oldest to move back after college and her middle child to decide to commute from home when she entered college next fall. Foreseeing those circumstances, she might have moved to something bigger.

Three closet-sized bedrooms housed the kids down one hallway, but another, much larger bedroom had been built off the side of the kitchen for the newlyweds. Dameon always called it "The Palace" because of the size of the room and its private bathroom. The living room opened into the kitchen with a divider wall of cupboards that stood chesthigh. When the bedroom was added on, two walls of glass were added on as well to create an atrium-like dining room off the back of the kitchen

" 'Sup," Dax said as Parker entered the living room. His stepdad was sprawled out on the sofa, his laptop resting on his stomach. "Rough night last night?"

"Nah," Parker replied. "Just late."

"Your mom thinks you were drinking," he commented.

Parker shuffled his feet into the kitchen and opened the refrigerator, searching for the first thing that caught his eye. "Yeah, I know. She told me."

"Were you?"

"Would you believe me if I told you no?" He found a hardboiled egg in the door's egg holder and shook it by his ear.

"Probably not."

"Then why bother asking me?" Parker retorted. He held up the egg. "Is this any good?"

"Dameon made them yesterday. I think he's saving that one. You probably ought to find something else."

Parker put the egg back and continued to rummage through the leftovers. "Well, I wasn't," he said, for no other reason than his own satisfaction. "And I take offense at the notion that I was."

"Your mother just gets worried at times," Dax explained. "It doesn't help the way you stay out 'til all hours, and we don't even know who you're with. And then there's this chop-job on your head this morning."

"There's nothing to worry about. There's nothing going on. I have better things to do than drink. Just because I came in late and slept late doesn't mean a thing. And just because I got sick of my hair doesn't mean I cut it while I was high or something."

Dax laughed. "Back off, tiger. It's no big deal. Just keep your head on, and don't do anything stupid."

Parker settled on a bowl of cereal and joined his stepdad in the living room.

Listen, Dax. What do you really know about Jesus? Do you know that

He died for you? Do you know how much He loves you?

Of course, that conversation with Dax would never happen. He'd never listen, and he'd never understand that Parker had found truth in the one place Dax was positive there was no truth in. So, instead, they'd sit here and talk about meaningless stuff.

Dax closed the screen on his laptop and sat up, swinging his legs to the floor. "What do you know about the local indie music scene?"

Scooping a spoonful of cereal into his mouth, Parker shrugged his shoulders. "Seen a few good bands around, I guess," he mumbled between mouthfuls.

"I'm trying to get something on this band."

"What band?" Parker asked, trying to keep his hand steady as he brought the spoon back to the bowl.

"It's a Christian band called Second Rate," he said, shuffling a stack of papers in front of him on the coffee table. "They're the headliner at the block party. You ever heard of them? I heard they're kids. They probably go to your school."

Parker tried to act surprised. "They any good?"

"They're Christian!" Dax snorted.

"I've heard there's some pretty sweet Christian bands out anymore, Dax," he replied.

Again, Dax snorted. "Sure there are. Like POD and Creed are Christian, right? Grabbing at straws again are all they're doing. Someone sings a song that sounds spiritual and they snatch them up as Christian. I know that there are just as many people out there that don't believe those two bands are Christian as there are people who do." He turned his attention back to the papers in his hand.

Shrugging his shoulders again, Parker dove back into his cereal. If he really wanted to start an argument, all he'd have to do was bring up the number of guitarist awards Phil Keaggy had won throughout the years, but that fact might lead to more questions than Parker was willing to answer right now.

Parker's eyes kept wandering back to the papers. He wanted to know so badly what information his stepdad held in his hands. Was there anything in there that was going to give him away? Or did Dax already know?

Maybe I should come clean now.

"The thing I don't get," Dax said softly, "is this: How does a band get a headliner gig when I don't even know about them? I'm *Dax at Night*! I know everything there is to know about the local indie scene, including a few bands that are all about that Jesus movement. Beatniks singing about God is all they are." He shook the papers in front of him. "This band gets a major gig, and there is nothing for them anywhere. No MP3s. No Web site, nothing! So who are they, and what are they hiding? How'd they just go and get a gig like this if it's not some kind of political move?"

Parker continued eating his cereal, hoping Dax wouldn't push with the questions. He didn't want to lie to him anymore.

"I tell you what," Dax continued. "I'm going to get to the bottom of this. There's no reason for a band that professes a faith of any kind to be playing at a government-sanctioned, public event. I'm going to find out who this band is and who's behind all this. And we're going to stop them, Parker. They are not going to be getting on that stage."

CHAPTER 114

Parker started to run, his board tucked under his arm, down the empty street toward the pizza shop. His house was smothering him—they were choking the life out of him, and they weren't even aware they were doing it. As his chest began to burn from the exertion, he could feel hope coming back. The farther he got from home, the better he felt. Soon he would be with his friends and hope would be in their midst as well.

Still running at full speed, he tossed the board on the ground in front of him and hopped on cleanly. When he was eight, he broke his nose after falling headfirst off his board while trying that very trick for the first time. People didn't understand how difficult it really was. Now it was one of Parker's favorites—a king's trick reserved for the best of the best. He loved the speed and adrenaline rush that came with knowing one false move meant he'd be kissing pavement.

That adrenaline rush had a lot to do with his love for skating as a whole, but there was more to it than just the fear factor. Skating was an art form.

The plan was to find Elijah before he left his shift at Angelino's. Parker wasn't sure if he was going to tell him everything about Dax, but he did want to break the news that his stepdad was going to try to shut down their big gig. He knew he needed to. The truth was going to come out eventually, and Parker wanted it to be him that told them about Dax.

Unfortunately, letting them know who Dax was really wasn't going to do anything to save their show.

They had to come up with a strategy.

I wonder if the rest of them will go for the sex, drugs, and rock 'n' roll thing?

He laughed aloud at the thought of it. That's what he had to do—talk them into playing "Stairway to Heaven," and all would be well. Pastor Terry probably wouldn't be too crazy about that choice of covers.

A car honk startled him as it sped by. Parker moved over as close to the curb as he could get while still pumping his leg to keep his momentum. People in town were actually pretty tolerant of the skaters. Only on occasion did someone yell at them or complain to the paper about them skating on the streets. Horror stories from some of the surrounding towns and local crackdowns on the sport ran rampant through the area skate cliques. Skaters in Parker's town didn't have to deal with that. It was just one more reason Parker liked living here. In fact, he thought more people needed to appreciate the art form of skating.

Parker kicked up his board into his hand as he waited at a stoplight. The sun was beating down on his neck, and he could feel his skin scorching. There were only two more blocks 'til he reached the pizza shop. The shirt had to go. He wasn't sure what made him decide to wear two in the first place. He yanked the navy polo over his head and tucked it into the back of his shorts, letting it hang loose over his hip.

"Hey!" he heard a voice from across the street call. A girl with braids sticking out from under an old school baseball cap with a white-mesh back and red bill stood holding onto the light post. Shanice was dressed in her favorite pair of army green pants cut off mid-calf, a red tank top, and her in-line skates, and she was waving wildly.

He dropped the board and skated across the street to her. "Hey, 'Nice. Whatcha doing?" He snatched the hat off her head and placed it on his own.

She grabbed the hat back. "What happened to your hair?" she asked, bouncing her hand off the tips of his stiff 'do.

"You like it?" He took the hat back, readjusting it to fit his head.

"It's going to take some getting used to. I almost didn't recognize you. What's up with that?"

Parker shrugged. "I just needed something different."

"It's different for you, that's for sure," she said honestly. "You in your own world today? I was chasing you for blocks." He spun out of her way as she tried to retrieve the hat. "Give me back my hat. My hair's all crazy."

"Girl, your hair don't look any different than it ever does," he said sweetly. He clapped the hat back on the top of her head.

"Where you heading at mach speed?"

Pointing down the street, Parker shrugged. "See if anyone was at the shop, I guess. Just out and about. If I would have known you were trying to catch me, I would have slowed down."

The walk light lit up, and they both crossed the street. Parker tucked the board under his arm, walking beside her.

"Well, aren't you just a bundle of joy today," she quipped.

"It's the show and all. Just freakin' over it," Parker blurted. "Nothing, really." He mounted the board again.

"You think he's gonna get his way and get us removed?" she asked.

"He's pretty persuasive when he wants to be, and he's not one to just sit back when it comes to church and state stuff."

"You sound like you know him or something," Shanice said dismissively.

"Or something," he replied before kicking a perfect ollie over the parking lot curb.

"We'll just fight fire with fire, I guess."

"You think it's going to be that easy?" Parker asked, picking up his skateboard and opening the door to the pizza shop for his friend.

She nodded. "I didn't say it was going to be easy, but we'll win out in the end. 'Cuz God has a plan for us to do big things with this band, remember?" She smiled at the notion of turning his own frequently used words on him. "You watch and see. We'll be at the show."

CHAPTER 15

The tall, thin Italian behind the counter nodded in greeting to the pair as they entered the shop. A telephone was planted to his ear with a second one ringing at his side. Three o'clock in the afternoon, and the pizzas were already flying out the door. He tucked his hand over the receiver and asked them as they crossed the room, "Need something to drink, guys?"

Parker shook his head. "No thanks, Mr. Angelino. We're looking for 'Lijah."

"Sent him out of here twenty minutes ago because we were so dead," Mr. Angelino replied after hanging up the phone. He rested his hand on the other receiver and took a deep breath. "And now look at us."

"Do you need some help?"

"No, no, he was heading to one of the girls' houses to do band stuff. That boy just eats, sleeps, and lives for your band."

Parker and Shanice traded smiles. "I can relate," Shanice said happily.

"Get some pizza or go play!" the cook exclaimed with a grin of his own. "Out with you!"

With a final wave, the two left.

As they were crossing the parking lot, Mr. Angelino emerged from the store. "I forgot, someone was here today asking questions about you!" he called.

Parker hurried back to him, glancing around the parking lot for any signs of Dax or any of his radio station guys who might be lurking nearby. "For me?"

"For the band, actually," he replied, wiping his hands on the sauce-stained apron around his waist.

Shanice piped in. "Who was it?"

"Didn't get a name."

Parker ran his fingers through his hair, his heart going full speed. "Did he say what he wanted?"

"Wasn't a he," the old man began before shaking his head. "Two girls. They said they needed to know the name of the band that played here all the time. I told them they needed to come back when the missus was here because I didn't even remember your name." He looked thoughtfully at the sky for a moment. "Come to think of it, I don't think you kids ever told me what you named that band."

"Probably just some fans," Shanice muttered, punching Parker on the arm. "Chicks looking for you."

Letting a sigh escape, Parker nodded slowly. "Can you do me a favor, Mr. Angelino?"

"Anything, my boy!"

"If anyone else comes around asking stuff, can you let us know right away? Don't tell them anything, just let us know."

"There's stuff going down," Shanice added, looking at Parker, "and we don't want to see you get dragged into anything ugly. It wouldn't be fair at all to you."

The pizza maker bobbed his head. "The whole thing in the paper, right?"

Parker jolted again. "The paper?"

"Some clown wrote a letter to the editor complaining about you guys being in the block party. You didn't read it yet?"

Parker laid his head in defeat on Shanice's shoulder. He never read the paper. What if Dax signed his name? If Dax wrote it, Parker was sure that his name was on it. Everything was done with an intent to get publicity for Dax.

It's over. They're going to know now.

They were sure to know that he was related to Parker when they found out Dax's last name.

"Was it that Dax guy?" Shanice asked. "From the radio station?"

Mr. Angelino waved an arm dismissively. "Oh, I don't know who it was. Cec took it back home, and she's writing the newspaper her own letter right now, let me tell you. I'm sure she's tearing up whoever wrote it." The phone started ringing inside. "I need to go get that. You go on over. Cec has the paper."

The teens sprinted across the lawn to the back door of the Angelino house. Christian talk radio greeted them at the screen door. From the kitchen table, the stout woman motioned them to come in just as Shanice was about to knock.

"My poor babies," she cooed. "I can't believe this stuff. Did you read this?"

Parker took the paper from her outstretched hand and pulled a chair out from the table. Shanice leaned over his shoulder to read. Closing his eyes momentarily, Parker whispered a prayer of thanks when he saw the letter writer's name: Thomas Roberts, Freethinkers Association.

He scanned through the letter quickly. There was a bunch of rhetoric about constitutional rights, freedom from religious indoctrination, and threats of a boycott of the businesses that would continue to support the block party through "this outright endorsement of Christian idealism by agreeing to the choice of a religious form of entertainment."

"I wrote in my letter that I don't need any 'freethinkers' coming down and eating my pizza," Mrs. Angelino said, pointing at that section of the letter. "How 'bout I put a big sign in my window that says, YOU DON'T LIKE CHRIST? THEN DON'T EAT HERE! See how they like that."

"I don't know how Christian that is, Mrs. Angelino," Shanice replied, "but I'm sure it felt good to write it."

She slapped the table as she laughed. "You know me, Shanice. I'll take it out before I send it. Why do these people have to cause trouble for such good kids? Why do grown men feel they have to raise a fuss about some kids playing music for an hour?"

Studying the letter, Parker shrugged his shoulders. He didn't know Thomas Roberts, but he was sure Dax did. The Freethinkers Association sounded like an organization Dax would be a part of. "Some of them think it's their duty," he replied.

"Their duty is to ruin a clean, good time for kids?"

"Well, they see their duty as protecting others from having religious beliefs forced on them."

"I don't have a problem with someone's right to walk into a building and subject himself to brainwashing," Dax had said to him once, "but I will do what I can to stop them from bringing it into the streets and taking away others' rights not to be brainwashed."

"Well, the Constitution also affords me some rights," Shanice said firmly. "It says 'freedom *of* religion,' not 'freedom *from* religion.' I have as much right to speak my mind as they do."

"Yes, you do," Mrs. Angelino said, patting her on the arm, "and so do I. That's why I will give them my own letter. People need to see that we're not going to stand for this."

"We've still got over two weeks 'til the show," Parker said, folding the paper up. He handed it back to Mrs. Angelino. "I'm sure this will all blow over before then."

"We'll just have to pray that it does." She waved the paper in the air and shook her head. "Because those blowhards don't want me after them."

CHAPTER 16

Downtown's scene mirrored most Midwestern county seats. A stone courthouse surrounded by old cannons and memorials to the area's past war veterans towered over a good number of two- and three-story buildings. Many of the storefronts were in various stages of renovation thanks to a recent revitalization effort to save downtown from the mighty suburban shopping mall. That had been one of Dax's rare non-religious-issue coups. An area philanthropist had donated money to spearhead the changes after hearing Dax speak on the need to keep the town's shopping area part of the cultural center of the area.

A tiny bookstore with an open courtyard in front of it sat across from the courthouse in a building with two other businesses. Shading a welcoming park bench, a red-and-green-striped awning flapped in the wind. A small fountain with a cherubic Roman boy holding a cracked pot overlooked three whimsically designed wrought-iron tables with chairs. Flowering clematis and ivy engulfed the base of the fountain and threatened to take over the block-stone walkway as well. Bright red flowers and two white birch trees filled the back corner of the courtyard. A brown and green painted sign in old-world lettering said "BOOKS & SUCH" above the door of the shop.

"Hey, guys!" a girl with reddish brown hair pulled into a ponytail called from an open window on the third floor. "We're up here. Come on up."

Eight months ago, Amber Smith might as well have melted into the walls. She was yet another nameless face in a school full of faces Parker didn't care to name. She fit in everywhere and nowhere at the same time. Though Parker hated to think it, he knew that had things been different—had he not come to Christ when he did—he would never have known her. He didn't like being reminded of the person he was before, a guy who wouldn't give a girl a second look if she didn't "fit in."

When Elijah had first pointed her out, Parker laughed. To a boy raised on the notion that music equated flamboyance, it was inconceivable to him that she, Amber, could be from a musical family. This girl's father couldn't possibly be a studio musician who split his time between Nashville and Los Angeles playing with a number of great acts. Fashion seemed the least of her interests, and her thick curly hair seldom came out of its ponytail. She walked through the halls clutching her books tight to her chest and never saying a word to anyone.

Parker followed Shanice around the alley to the back of the building. Two narrow wooden decks ran the length of the hall on the second and third stories with more flowers and greenery hanging from them. A little touch of New Orleans in Ohio, Parker always thought when he saw it.

Parker bounded up the stairs two at a time as Shanice sat down to remove her skates. "Hey, let's get this party started!" He burst through the door and threw his arms in the air.

"Too bad it's already here," Andria retorted, tossing a dish towel at him. "Liking the 'do, guy."

He touched his hair and smiled. "Thanks." With a jump backward, he let the towel fall to the floor in front of him. "But if this party has anything to do with doing dishes, I'm so out of here."

The kitchen, like most of the aging apartment, was decorated in a warm and friendly fashion with an overabundance of birdhouses and sunflowers. Darby and Andria sat at either ends of the table, plates of macaroni and cheese in front of them, and Amber leaned against the yellow-tiled counter with a bowl of pasta in hand. Cross-legged on the floor, Elijah raised a fork in greeting and dug back into playing with the food in front of him.

Shanice entered in stocking feet and let the metal screen door bang loudly behind her. "That felt good," she giggled. Banging screen doors was one of her mother's pet peeves. "I thought we were making music here?"

"Hey, a man's gotta eat," Elijah retorted.

"Man?" Shanice studied the room from one end to the other. "I see no man here."

"Oh, booger off. I was going to share my mac 'n' cheese with you, but now you've insulted me, so you can watch me eat."

Darby spun around to face Parker, who was still standing in the doorway. "Where's Jenna Rose?"

"Why do you think I would know? Huh?" Parker wrapped his arms around her head in a headlock and pretended to twist. "And get that smirk off your face."

"I just thought if anyone would know. . ." Darby wrapped an arm around his neck and pinched his cheek.

"Well, I don't know anything."

"We gotta get Jenna over here," Shanice said. "We can't have a band meeting without her."

Amber had the phone in her hand. "I had no idea everyone was coming over, or I would have told her, too. What's her number?"

Darby reached for the phone. "I'll do it. I call her all the time." As a smile spread across her face, she held the phone out to Parker. "Unless you want to?"

"Man, you guys all need to quit it!" As Darby stood up from the table, Parker grabbed her plate. "Snooze you lose," he sang, feeding himself with his fingers.

"I sneezed all over that," she said solemnly. Another wide smile crossed her face as she put the receiver to her ear.

He returned the smile and shuffled more food into his mouth. The cheese dripped from his fingers. "I thought it had a little something— something to it."

Andria groaned and pushed her plate across the table. "You are both so gross."

Parker put the plate back down on the table and licked his fingers. "Uh, no thanks," he countered. "I'm too full to eat any more."

"You wanna finish mine?" Elijah asked, holding up his still nearly full bowl.

Parker kicked at him. "What'd we miss?"

"Just everything!" Elijah scooted across the floor and handed his dishes to Amber. "My compliments to the chef, but I'm stuffed."

Darby hung the phone back on the wall. "Her dad's bringing her over in a few."

"Did you guys know we made the paper?" Shanice asked. "And it's not a good thing." She relayed the story to them.

"I still think it's going to just blow over," Parker commented. He pulled a paper towel from the wall holder and finished cleaning his hands. Still with his back to the others, he let his eyes fall close and muttered the words "I hope" to the end of the statement.

"Maybe we should call Pastor Terry and see where he stands on this," Elijah said.

"Since he's a *minister*, I'd like to think we know what his stand would be," said Darby.

"But he's the one who contacted us, right?" Amber asked. Up to her elbows in soapsuds, she turned around long enough to ask her question and then got back to cleaning the dishes.

"Yeah." Parker nodded. "But he's not the guy in charge of the whole event. I think he was the one who knew about us and then called the committee."

Andria carried the two plates to the sink and dunked them in the water. She scooped up a pile of bubbles and blew them at Elijah. "But he's still our guy, right? He's the one who contacted us, so we need to be contacting him if we have any questions. That's how this whole thing works, isn't it?"

"So who is in charge?" Darby asked.

"The park and recreation guy," Elijah said, shrugging his shoulders, "if anyone knows who that is."

"Let's call Pastor Terry and see what his thoughts are," Darby said. She had the phone in her hand again. "Someone look up the number for me."

"Just ask him if we can come down and talk to him," Parker suggested. Digging through the phone book, he tried not to look up as Jenna Rose walked in the door. "I'd rather do it in person. I want to know if this committee is at our back or if they're going to cave if the pressure gets heavy from these people."

"Oh, I see," Jenna Rose said while trying to look upset, "you guys are having a party without me."

Parker pointed at the number in the book. "There it is."

"It kinda just happened," Amber said apologetically. "Everybody just showed up. Mom's at work, and a couple of us were going to work on some music, and it just grew."

"Oh, it's no big deal." Jenna Rose laughed. "What are we doing?"

"Maybe we should pull out of the show," Darby said. She grabbed Jenna Rose around the shoulder and gave her a squeeze. "We made the paper. More stuff questioning us being at the block party."

"Why?" her sister demanded. "Why should we pull out and admit defeat before there's even a real fight? No way."

Darby tucked her long bangs behind her ears. "I think the whole thing stinks, but the block party is the highlight of the summer for a lot of people, and I don't want to see us ruin it with all this controversy."

"We're not ruining anything, Darb," Elijah said, patting her on the leg. "*Dax at Night* and his cronies are the ones trying to ruin it."

Jenna Rose wrapped her arms around Darby's shoulders from behind and hugged her back. "Besides, in the music biz, a little controversy never hurt anyone. The more *Dax at Night* puts our name in the spotlight, the better. That's how this game is played."

The more they talked about Dax, the more Parker felt like an outsider to them. He watched their conversation intently, waiting for the moment when someone would point a finger at him and say, "And he's your dad!"

Jenna Rose's gaze on the back of his neck was nearly as hot as the afternoon sun, but Parker continued to fumble with the phone book. He would do just about anything to occupy himself instead of facing her in front of everyone else. Darby scooted over, offering half of her chair to the newcomer as she dialed the number. Jenna Rose took the seat next to him instead and jabbed his elbow as she took her seat. Parker smiled and poked her back, still unsure about looking at her. What was she going to say? And, more importantly, where was she hoping things would go from here?

"We need to talk," she leaned over and whispered.

He nodded in reply, unable to voice the thought racing through his mind: *four of the worst words in the English language.*

CHAPTER 17

I could use another lesson," Jenna Rose said, falling in beside Parker.

Smiling, he shifted the board tucked under his arm and continued to walk silently.

"I see," she replied, letting her eyes focus on her feet. She watched them for a dozen or so steps.

Parker let out a deep sigh and fought back the urge to start running, drop his board, and go for it, whether it be glory or face-diving. He didn't know what to say—he didn't even know what he *wanted* to say.

But he did know that however the conversation was going to go, it didn't need to happen in front of everyone else.

The trek to the small nondenominational church and Pastor Terry's office was nearly ten blocks away. Parker was second-guessing his decision to walk it with everyone else instead of using his board. And was it his imagination, or was everyone else staying just far enough ahead so the two of them could fall back at the end and have a bit of privacy? They seemed just as determined that he and Jenna Rose get together as he seemed to be in keeping himself single.

"Are you not talking?" she asked.

"What do you want me to say?"

"I want you to say what you're thinking."

Why do girls always ask that? "I don't know what I'm thinking," he replied. "I'm still trying to figure out what I'm thinking." He chuckled in frustration, rubbing the top of his head with his free hand. "When I figure out what I'm thinking, I'll be sure to let you know."

"Yeah," she said, bringing her eyes up from her feet and staring ahead intently, "thanks for the *lesson*, I guess."

The hurt and anger in her tone stung his ears and tore at his heart. The malice behind the word *lesson* made it obvious that she was talking about a lot more than the skating tips.

Now look what you've gone and done, dork. The last person you ever wanted to hurt, and you just stomped on her, too. He was treating her no differently than any of the others, right?

"Sometimes you can't just hide from who you really are, can you?" he muttered to himself as he dropped his board and skated into the street.

With each pump of his leg, he gained speed, leaving the others walking far behind.

He was the king of the wind and the road and the wheel—just like when he first started skating at age seven. The red-carpet road before him was his path alone. Ordinary folks walked the sidewalks.

One glance over his shoulder revealed Jenna Rose with her arms crossed tightly over her chest. Surrounded by Shanice and Darby, her pace had slowed even more. Darby had her arm around her.

Parker pumped his leg harder and faced straight ahead.

The wide, shaded front stoop of the old brick church offered a welcome spot for Parker after his heavy workout. Parker plopped down and leaned his chin on the tail of his board. Spinning the wheels mindlessly, he kept his eyes on the road in front of them. The others were nowhere in sight.

He forgot how long it took the commoners to travel by foot.

A short man with salt-and-pepper hair and a bushy moustache opened the church door. "You need anything, friend?" Pastor Terry studied Parker for a moment and added, "Take a break for as long as you need. The drinking fountain right inside the door is just as cold as anything you're going to buy at the gas station across the street."

Parker nodded and thanked him.

Pastor Terry scanned the street in front of the church. "Oh, I'm sorry. I know you. Where are your friends? You're part of that band, aren't you?"

Parker pointed down the sidewalk to the group that was now barely in view. "I skated to meet them here. They're on their way."

"Well, you're welcome to come on inside and meet them in here. It's much cooler."

With another glance down the street, Parker shook his head. "Thanks anyway, Pastor. I'll wait for the rest."

"Just remember what I said about that drinking fountain," he said with a wink, letting the door close behind him.

Parker wanted to ask him to stay and talk, but he wasn't sure what he expected the minister to do for him. He wasn't really sure if there was anything anyone could do for him—these were problems it looked like he was going to have to handle on his own.

As his friends drew closer, he could see Jenna Rose still hanging to the back of the group with Darby and Shanice, but now they were laughing, their arms linked around each other.

It wasn't fair to think that she should still be upset, but Parker did feel a bit of sadness that she seemed to be over it so quickly. But the last thing he wanted was to make her upset. She had a right to her own feelings.

He jumped to his feet and left his board on the steps. "What took you so long?" he said lightly.

"Why'd you weird out on us and take off?" Elijah asked.

"I just needed to think." He wiped his forehead as he looked at Jenna Rose. Her eyes were on her feet again. Biting his lip in defeat, he pointed at the building behind him. "Pastor Terry is waiting on us."

The inside of the tiny church was nothing like Faith Calvary Temple. At their church, everything in the main part of the building was very formal and ornate. Upon entering, one knew he had entered a place of worship. Pastor Terry's church, on the other hand, felt like a community center or day care with its brightly colored bulletin boards and posted messages everywhere. Collection boxes for canned goods, baby items, and clothing lined one wall. Parker studied the assorted flyers and notices as they waited for the pastor. This church functioned much like a community center according to the notes he saw—CPR classes, tutoring, after-school clubs, a food pantry, and seniors' luncheons. It was no wonder the minister and congregation took such an active role in the block party preparations and other outreach activities. Parker decided Faith Calvary could probably learn a lot from this place.

The pastor ushered them into his office and took a seat behind the desk. "What can I do for you?" Parker and Elijah sat in the wingback chairs facing the desk while the girls stood, leaning against the wall.

Elijah explained their concerns. The pastor listened closely, nodding at times and once jotting a note in the notebook in front of him.

"We wanted your thoughts, Pastor," Jenna Rose added when Elijah was finished. "Should we back out from the show?"

"Well, I hope you don't," he said, closing the notebook and placing it in a drawer. He tapped his pen in front of him as he looked over the group. "But I think that's a question that can only be answered in prayer. Are you thinking of backing down because it would be best for the party or for yourselves?"

Parker rubbed his face with both hands and said nothing as his friends murmured back and forth. He didn't understand what they were discussing—they all knew it was the personal scrutiny that they didn't want—backing out of the party was about protecting themselves. No one had said anything about what was best for the block party. Now that he thought of it, Parker realized they hadn't even given a thought about how this was going to affect the party or those who had planned it.

"There are a lot of people backing this block party," Pastor Terry continued, "and they were all in agreement that they wanted good, clean entertainment that would draw in young people without scaring off the families pushing strollers. Remember, for every individual protester, there are ten people who are in support of you being our band."

"Why isn't that in the paper?" Shanice asked.

"Because the media has selective hearing when it comes to Christians," Elijah interjected. "We could all write our own letters, and I'm sure they won't make it in print."

"Do you think we should play secular music?" Parker asked.

Elijah bolted from his seat. "Are you serious? There's no way we can learn a whole new set in two weeks. Man, who are you?"

"Plus," Shanice said, shaking her head, "that would be totally compromising who we are. We might as well not stand for anything."

"It was just a suggestion," Parker snapped.

Darby stood up and walked between the two friends. "We could maybe do one. We have enough time to learn one. I mean, we don't want to exclude anyone."

"Like what?" Elijah asked, still shaking his head.

"How 'bout 'Stairway to Heaven'?" Parker mumbled.

"What?"

"Nothing."

"Man, what is up with you today?" Elijah paced in front of the window.

"Nothing," Parker said again.

"Nothing? Yeah, right. Man, we're all stressing over this."

"You have no idea," Parker replied.

All eyes were trained on him—even the pastor's.

Here's my chance. I can come clean and tell them all the stuff I've been neglecting to tell them for the past eight months. They deserve to know who Dax is and how when he finds out about me being in this, Second Rate may be minus one guitar player. It's time to face the music.

"Well, try us," Jenna Rose stated, annoyance evident in her voice.

Parker took a deep breath and bit his lip as he exhaled slowly. "Forget it. You know, it was a dumb idea. We need to just keep things the way they are. It works the way it is, and that's that."

The way they were before last night. Understand that?

Holding his focus, Jenna Rose licked her lips and drew in her own breath.

As the others thanked him and filed out of his office, the pastor turned to Parker. "May I speak with you for a moment?" he asked kindly.

Parker nodded and gestured to the others to go ahead without him. He had his skateboard; catching up would be no problem.

Pastor Terry circled around his desk and sat in one of the wingback chairs. He motioned for Parker to sit in the other one. As Parker sat down, he asked, "Is there something more, Parker? I haven't known you long, but I remember you being much more jovial and so excited about this opportunity before. Is there something more on your mind that you'd like to talk about?"

Rubbing the side of his face, Parker stared at his feet. What was he supposed to say? What could he tell him?

"You seem much more reserved than I first suspected. Maybe I'm wrong. . ."

"No, sir, you're probably not," Parker replied.

"Well, son, Christ Himself was persecuted, and He reminds us that we are no better than our Master. You guys can choose to step away from this controversy. I don't think anyone would fault you for it." Clapping Parker on the back, he stood up and walked to the window. "Or you can choose to make music and have a ministry. But if you want a ministry, you can't let persecution shut you down. It's up to you."

"What if the persecution is coming from people close to you?"

"In the book of Matthew, chapter ten, it says, 'Brother will betray brother to death, and a father his child; children will rebel against their parents. . . . All men will hate you because of me, but he who stands firm to the end will be saved.' Does that sound to you like Christ expected it to be easy for us to be Christians?"

"Christ never said it would be easy," Parker mumbled.

"That's right, He said quite the opposite. A lot of people just haven't stepped out of their comfort zone to experience life like Christ warned us about."

"Thanks, Pastor," Parker said, getting to his feet. "Thanks for your support and everything."

Pastor Terry nodded. "Remember, Parker, Second Rate is a fine musical act. You're good, clean, fun entertainment, and there's nothing wrong with that. There's not enough out there. But if you want to truly serve God, you have to surrender yourself completely to Him. That means accepting the good and the bad. That's the only way you're going to be a ministry. But if you want to stay just a band, there's nothing wrong with that either."

CHAPTER 18

The short stairway stretched into what seemed like miles. Parker stood and listened to the sound of the pool balls shuffle around the table as his brother played a game.

The decision to get Dameon's input had been a difficult one. Parker knew what Corrina thought of his newfound faith. Asking her for advice on how to talk to Dax would likely prove an unproductive way to spend his afternoon. However, a whole world separated the two brothers as far as their ages. Their relationship was not your typical big-brother-little-brother bond. Dameon never had time for his youngest sibling, and Parker always viewed Dameon as someone standing just beyond his grasp—an enigma he would never understand but would always be tied to through blood. Dameon was a role model, even someone Parker looked up to. However, Parker looked up to Tony Hawk too. But the truth was Dameon was no more accessible than the skating superstar was.

Parker was fairly certain talking to his mom would be equally disastrous. She weathered her way through Dax's tantrums for years until the news that her ex-husband was a changed man thanks to his new church-going wife. Suddenly she had plenty to say about religious people. And, of course, Dax just fed off her rage on that subject. Together they were a lethal combination.

As for Dameon, Parker had no idea where he stood with religion. Dameon, like everyone else in the Blevins household, did his own thing.

Where Christ fit into the picture for his older brother was uncertain. Like himself, Parker knew that Dameon looked up to Dax. While in college, his brother had followed in his stepdad's footsteps numerous times by protesting religious activities on campus.

But he could change. Parker had.

"Please lead me to say what You want me to say, Lord," he whispered as he started down the steps. "Take me out of my comfort zone."

His brother lifted his chin in greeting and returned his attention to the shot at hand. Dameon was twenty-four, but he looked much older with his neatly trimmed goatee and short business-style haircut. He hardly looked anything like the mohawk-wearing skater punk that turned his baby brother onto the sport. "Hey, Curly-locks, what's up?"

"Wanna game?" Parker asked, finding the other pool stick.

"You up for getting beat?" Dameon replied. He began shuffling the balls into the rack.

"By you? As if."

"Well, you can talk smack," Dameon said with a smile. "But let's see if you can back it. If you still can't play any better than you used to, just get back upstairs, because you're wasting my time."

Parker smiled in anticipation. For the first time in months, life in his house felt normal again.

"Any luck with the job hunt?" Parker regretted the words almost as quickly as he said them.

"I just need to come to an acceptance that I'm the most highly educated stock boy on the planet, that's all," his brother replied. Dameon leaned on the stick, reduced to little more than a shell of what he once was. Parker could remember him coming home from college. The air of confidence around him permeated his every move. When Dameon Blevins walked into a room, he commanded attention, and people were naturally drawn to his intelligence and quick wit. Long before he even knew Dax Blevins existed, Parker wanted to be his big brother.

And now you could be the one counseling him. What's wrong with this picture?

"You just got to be patient, that's all." The balls separated with a loud crack. A solid red ball rolled lazily into the corner pocket. His second shot didn't fare as well.

"Is this what you've been doing with all your time?" Dameon asked. "Playing pool?"

"Not exactly."

"Yeah, Mom thinks you're doing drugs."

Parker broke into laughter, thumping his head on the tabletop. "She thinks you are, too."

Dameon flicked the end of Parker's pool stick, causing the tip to graze across the top of the cue ball. In one quick motion, Parker swung the stick like a baseball bat over his brother's head.

"So, you're doing as much as I am, huh?" Dameon asked. He bounced his shoulder against Parker and smiled.

"If that number is zero."

Parker stepped back to give him room to take his shot.

"So," Dameon said, "you're not playing pool and you're not doing drugs. So what are you doing with all your time? You got a girl out there or something you aren't telling us about?"

"Man, just take your shot," Parker grumbled, but he felt like his chance to talk seriously with his brother was slipping away. "Everything in my life is not about girls."

"Nah, now it's about Jesus," Corrina giggled as she turned the corner into the rec room. She crossed the room and plopped down on the brown leather sofa. "Better watch yourself, Dameon. He might try to convert you."

"Get out of here, Cori," Parker ordered. He snatched a pillow from the loveseat and threw it at her.

"What? I'm not worthy of saving?"

"If you're just going to make fun of me, get out of here."

Corrina stretched a leg out and touched her big brother on the knee with her toe. "You believe this, Dameon? He's going to leave me to just rot in hell instead of showing me the light."

Parker's heart sank at the smile that crossed Dameon's face. "You're bad, Cori." He turned his attention back to the game and sank another shot. Lining the cue up for another, he glanced at Parker. "Look, doof, you can save your speech if you came down here to talk about Jesus."

"Why?" Parker blurted out. He blinked in surprise at his own boldness again. "What do you believe?"

"What I believe is none of your business."

"Have you ever read the Bible?"

"An old book of archaic rules? Jeez, Parker, don't tell me you've been sucked into that crap?" Dameon pushed past him to line up for his next shot. The playfulness in his movements was gone.

Parker licked his lips and tried to keep his eyes off his sister sitting there gleefully watching him squirm. "It's not just an old book of rules, Dameon. Man, you've got to read it. It's God's Word." He sighed and bit at his lip as he tried to gather his composure. "There is so much in there about how much God loves you."

"Wow, I had no idea," Corrina smirked, holding a hand over her mouth to keep from laughing. "It actually says, 'God loves Dameon' in it? Isn't Dameon like Satan or something?"

Dameon collapsed onto the table in laughter. "Girl, you are so wrong."

With each gasp of laughter from his eldest sibling, Parker felt himself quickly shrinking into the carpet. If only he really could just slink away into the walls unnoticed, he'd disappear completely. He would find his friends who didn't laugh at him for what he wanted to stand for.

"Seriously, doof. . ." Dameon faced him, the silliness gone from his face. "I don't want to be preached at, got it? I've read it, okay? I don't want to hear it. Leave me alone if all you want is to tell me about religion. I don't buy it."

"I wasn't trying to preach at you," Parker pleaded. "I wanted to hang out a bit. Just see how you were doing and all. I just wanted to talk a bit. See where you stood."

"I know where I stand. I stand on my own two feet. I make my own way in life, Parker," he stated, stuffing a finger into his younger brother's chest. "I don't need a crutch."

"I don't either, Dameon. I found the truth."

"Truth is something you can prove," his brother said sharply. He lined up to take another shot. "Where's your proof?"

Parker drew in a deep breath and whispered a quick prayer for guidance. If he only had one chance to say his piece, this was it. "In the Bible it says—"

"I don't care what the Bible says!" For the first time, Dameon's ball rattled around the hole and didn't go in. He stepped back so his brother could take his shot. "I don't believe the Bible is anything more definitive than *Moby Dick*. It's a *book*, Parker. You grew up in this house, too, didn't you? You should know better than anyone what Dax has always said about proof."

"Brainwashing," Corrina piped in.

Wringing his hands together, Parker glared at his sister. "Pull yourself together," he whispered to himself. He lined up his shot and missed terribly.

"If you can't tell me what you believe on your own, Parker," Dameon said, "then I don't want to hear what you believe." In one motion, he hit the eight ball in and let the stick drop on the table. "And you need to spend more time on your pool game before you start coming at me with smack."

CHAPTER 19

L et's do this," Parker urged, tearing into the powerful chords of the second song of their set.

Darby followed his lead, but the others stood still. Parker didn't care. He continued with the guitar riff and closed his eyes. Once she realized no one else was playing, Darby's sound faded out.

"Dude," Elijah said from what sounded like a million miles away. Parker ignored him. In the music, he was real. He wasn't lying to anyone, and he wasn't hiding anything about himself. When he was playing his guitar, he was exactly who he wanted to be.

The chord died as his power came to an abrupt stop.

Opening his eyes, Parker looked around at the others staring at him.

"That's the wrong song," Darby said. She shifted her guitar under her arm and walked closer to Parker. "What's up with you?"

"Nothing," he replied. "I needed to vent a bit. I figured you guys would just follow my lead."

"Man, why are you buggin'?" Shanice asked, fiddling with her microphone. "You've been wigging out on us for a few days now."

Parker hopped off the mock stage they had built in the practice room of Angelino's Pizzeria. Pulling the guitar strap over his shoulder, he held his instrument tightly in his hands as he found a seat. Fatigue was overcoming him. *Lord, I can't do this anymore. Give me the strength to do the right thing.*

"I think you guys ought to start shopping for a new guitarist," he said, his voice a hoarse whisper. A lump had settled itself tight in his throat, and he fought back tears. Second Rate was his idea—his work for his Savior, and it just didn't seem fair that his time with the band seemed to be coming to a close. Once Dax knew, Parker was sure his affiliation with the Christian rock band would be over. . .it was only a matter of time.

"Okay, you've more than weirded out," Elijah commented as he pulled a chair up beside his friend. He leaned forward on the back of the seat. "Start talking."

"Parker, there's no way we could replace you," Amber said. She grabbed another chair as everyone began clustering around the table.

Jenna Rose stood back, holding on to her microphone stand. "Parker, if this has anything to do with us—"

"Oh, come on, Jenna." He tried to sound lighthearted but instead it came out flat. "Okay, we kissed. It's not the end of the world."

Shanice grasped the sides of Parker's head with both hands and turned his face to look at her own. "Hold the bus! You guys did what?"

"You sure have been acting like it was the end of the world today," said Jenna Rose as she walked over to the group. Darby slung an arm over her shoulder.

"That's another conversation." Parker ran both hands through his hair and laid his head on the table. "You guys need to know something."

"If this has anything to do with the block party, dawg," Elijah said, patting him on the leg, "don't worry about it. You heard what Pastor Terry said. They aren't going to bow to the pressure and take us out of the show. We're going to tear that place up. Not even *Dax at Night* is going to have anything to say once he hears our sound. It's going to be fine."

Desperately, Parker held each one's gaze individually. These were his friends—friends like he never knew he could have, and he was the one who put this dream into their head. He had helped bring them together. Their dreams were on the brink of being realized, and he was not going to be with them to experience it.

"I haven't told you guys everything. It doesn't matter if we get to go on or not. When Dax finds out who we are, I won't be allowed to be in the group."

Andria patted him on the back. "Why? How can he do that?"

Parker lowered his head to the table again. Andria continued to rub his back. Ever so slightly, the insecurity began to melt away at her touch. He took a deep breath. It was time to face the music. "Because he's my stepdad."

CHHAPPTERR 220

Darby sat on the bench in front of the pizza shop, her feet out of her sandals and swinging back and forth. She grinned as Parker opened the door. "You thought you could just hang out until we all left, didn't you?"

"N–no," he stammered, letting the door close behind him. Blushing, he ducked his head. "Yeah, maybe."

She scooted over to give him room to sit next to her.

He sat down, gripping the edge of the seat with both hands. "I was just cleaning up the room some and thinking a bit. I wasn't ready to head home yet, but nobody seemed to want to hang out."

"You really threw us with that Dax news," she stated. "Why didn't you tell us before?"

"What'd you guys want me to say? 'Hi, my name is Parker, and I live with the loudmouth atheist on the radio?' I don't know. I just didn't know what you guys would think."

"I don't get why you'd think we'd think any less of you. You can't help who your family is."

Again, he shrugged his shoulders as his eyes watched his shuffling feet. He could feel her watching him. "Maybe I thought you guys would think I wasn't serious about this Christian thing or something."

She bumped her shoulder against him, allowing it to linger until he turned to look at her. "There's nothing you can say to change what we know about the way you love Christ, Parker. We can see it in you. It's there, and it's real, and nothing about the person you used to be or what you came from would change that. For any of us. Got that?"

He nodded as the smile crossed his face. Pushing her back with his own shoulder, he ran a hand over his head again. He wanted to show his appreciation—let her know how much the words meant to him, but he couldn't come up with the right thing to say. He could tell she knew by the way she bumped him back.

"So you kissed Jenna Rose." Darby was grinning like it was a good thing.

Parker gave her a light shove as he tried to hide his embarrassment. "She kissed me first," he retorted. "Twice. And then I kissed her. It was all pretty innocent, I think, but then again, it just makes a mess of everything. Total surprise to me. There's been a few times that I could tell she wanted me to kiss her, but she's never made a move before." He smiled in remembrance. "It was nice, but now everything's bound to be a mess."

"Why does it make a mess of everything?"

"Because it just does." Parker rested his chin in the palm of his hand.

"Well, you like her, right?"

"Yeah, a lot, and that's why it's all a mess."

Darby slipped her feet back into her sandals and stood up. "I don't get it. Why is it a mess?"

"How long have you known me?" he asked.

She sat back down on the bench, sideways this time, and crossed her legs in front of her. "I've known you long enough to know you don't normally act like this. We met in our guitar music elective last summer, right?" He nodded. "And I'd like to think in that time we've gotten to know each other pretty well."

"I'd say we have," he whispered.

"So, what is it you think you can't talk to me about?"

He let out a number of quick breaths and then spoke. "I don't know how much you know about my reputation. I'd like to say it was all a lie, but that wouldn't be truthful. I've played a lot of girls, Darby. I was a really different person before I got to know you."

"But you aren't that person anymore."

He snorted and shook his head. "I wish I could say he disappeared completely, Darby, but I have to fight him off every day." Hopping to his feet, he stepped into the parking lot and gave a rock a kick. It went skidding into the road. "I really like Jenna Rose, but I'm afraid I'm just going to become that other guy again. I'll make a move that leads her into something we're both going to regret, and it will mess everything up." He rubbed the side of his face and sighed again. "And besides, when she sees what I am, it's going to mess us up. It's going to mess the band up."

"You really did accept Christ, didn't you?" she asked, her gaze still intent on his face. "I know you did, Parker," she answered for him. "I can see Him in you. You're a new creation now. You're not that other guy anymore. You need to let what He did be your story."

Parker frowned. "I don't buy the whole born-again virgin thing, Darb. There are some things that knowing Christ won't undo."

"No, that's true," she agreed. "But God's forgiven you for it. Forgiven and forgotten. He's not going to hold it over your head. And I don't think Jenna Rose is going to either."

"I'm really afraid she will."

"You need to forgive yourself, too, Parker."

Parker snickered in embarrassment. Of course that had a lot to do with it.

But how can I forgive and forget when it's on my mind 24/7?

CHAPTER 21

P arker, may I talk to you?"

He sat up quickly at the soft tone of his mother's voice. "What's up?"

Seldom did she let down her guard. With teeth clenched, Parker kept himself from asking who had died. Whatever had brought this on had to be important, and in their family, that usually meant someone had died. His mom had been a good mom, but now that her children were nearly grown, she was ready to get on with her own life. Sometimes Parker sensed that he just wasn't growing up fast enough for her.

She leaned against the side of his bed and waited for him to take his headphones off. "I just got off the phone with your dad."

"Why are you talking to him?" He sat up in bed and let the book fall to the floor.

"I guess he talked to your sister yesterday." In a rare gesture of affection, she reached out and brushed a hand across his short hair. "I'm still not used to this," she mumbled with a weak smile. "He wants you to consider moving up with him," she said softly.

Parker jumped to his feet and stormed to the other side of his room. "Well, he can forget it." The foam ball in the corner received the brunt of his frustration. Parker was floored at the suggestion that he move up to Michigan to be with his dad's perfect new family.

"He hardly calls any of his three children back in Ohio more than once a month! And now all of a sudden he just decides I'm worthy of being part of his 'perfect' life? That's not going to happen, Mom."

"It's up to you," she said gently, "but I think it might not be a bad idea."

The floor seemed to drop out from under him. "Are you serious?" He stared at his mom in disbelief. *This from the woman who breaks out in hives at the mention of her ex-husband's name? What is happening?*

"He told me you've been going to church," she said.

"Yeah, and. . . ?" Corrina was so dead. She'd promised not to tell anyone. Obviously his dad had found out about this somehow. Parker really doubted it had anything to do with Dameon, since his brother still returned his dad's letters and refused to speak to him on the phone.

"I think I might actually agree with your dad that this might be best for you. Parker, why didn't you tell me you started going to church?"

Parker shrugged his shoulders. "I didn't know how you were going to react."

"I might have my own misgivings about religion, but I think it's a lot better than the alternatives."

"Like me doing drugs?" Parker laughed.

She smiled and touched her hand to her face in embarrassment. "Yeah, something like that. But I don't know what Dax is going to think of all this. His feelings run pretty strong when it comes to religion."

"You mean when it comes to Christianity, Mom."

"No, I mean religion."

Parker let out a snort. "No. Christianity. Can you ever recall him once picketing that New Age Renaissance Fair they hold in the park? Or shouting for boycotts on the Eastern religion class at the high school? When a local Wiccan group puts a float in the July Fourth parade, he touts the 'diversity' in town. But if a Christian youth group holds a car wash in the church's own parking lot, he goes on for days about them cramming their beliefs down other people's throats. His problem is with Christianity, Mom, not religion."

She stared at him for what seemed like hours. Parker could feel the lump in his throat start to return. He didn't want to hurt his mom, because he knew how much she cared for Dax, but he also knew these thoughts were the truth. He had been pushing these realizations down deep inside himself since he found Christ, but now that his secret was out, it wasn't going to be easy to sidestep the truth about Dax's biased feelings any longer.

Something awakened inside Parker at that moment. He remembered something Dax had drilled into their minds: "*When you're dealing with something you believe in, you don't beat around the bush. You just say it. Don't falter in what you believe. State yourself cleanly and boldly.*"

"Dax is strong in his beliefs for his own reasons, but he's a good man," his mother said defensively. "What he does is important."

"He fights for everyone's rights at the expense of Christians. Why don't I get the same rights he says everyone else deserves?"

She stood up, straightening the wrinkles in her slacks. The softness had drained from her eyes. "You have the same rights as the rest of us to believe what you want to believe, and he would argue that to his death. But I think that if you are going to seriously consider this 'Christian' thing, you might be best living with your dad. With Corrina's moodiness and Dameon's somberness, we don't need any more stresses in this house."

"I don't know why you think it needs to be any different than it has been, Mom. I've been going to church for almost a year now." Parker crossed the room and kicked the foam ball a second time.

"Yeah, and you've started acting so weird that I thought you were doing drugs for the past year. People don't just change overnight, but that's what you seemed to do."

"I pretty much did, Mom."

"Do you know what it will do to Dax to know this?" The touch of desperation in her voice caught him by surprise. He couldn't help but wonder who she was trying to protect by suggesting he go live with his dad—him or Dax.

"Would he like it better if I *were* doing drugs, Mom?" Parker was becoming more annoyed by the whole conversation.

"I'm just saying that he has a reputation to uphold, Parker. How's it going to look if his own son is against what he stands for? Did you think of that before you went into this phase?"

"It's not a phase, Mom. Dax says we should all be free to believe as we want to believe. If that doesn't include my right to believe as a Christian, then he's the one who's a hypocrite!"

She stormed to the door and turned back to face him. "I don't want to see you go, Parker Daniel, but if this is what you're going to stand for, I think you might be better living with your dad. You think about it. If this is a phase, get over it before you do irreparable damage to the work your stepfather has done. But if you believe this stuff for real, then I hope you consider being with your dad."

His board had once again brought Parker to her front door without his knowledge of the destination when he stepped on it. Still agitated from the conversation with his mom, he had hit the street and just started skating, 'til he got to Jenna Rose's house.

As he passed down the street the first time, he saw her sitting in that lawn chair, her legs pulled up to her chest in her favorite reading position and a book in her hand. At the sound of the wheels on pavement, her eyes left her page, and she rose to her feet waving him over. Considering his odd behavior the past three days since they had kissed, he was surprised she seemed so eager to spend time with him. He hadn't been the nicest guy he could have been since then.

"My mom thinks I should move to Michigan." Parker pulled on the legs of his baggy jeans as he sat down in the lawn chair on the Brinleys' front porch.

Jenna Rose was stretched out on the porch railing in front of him. "Are you serious?" she asked, her eyes wide.

He nodded and turned his attention to his shoes. The green Vans were covered with drawings and writing done mostly by himself and Shanice. The shoes really weren't that interesting—he was just trying to keep himself from staring at her stomach. Every time he looked at her, all his eyes were interested in was the smooth strip of skin peeking out between the hem of her shirt and her low-rise knit pants. "You know, I wish you wouldn't do that," he said.

"Do what?"

"Wear shirts like that."

She tossed her arms out to her sides and surveyed the blue jogging pants and white baby doll tee that stopped just above her navel. "What's wrong with it?"

"I have a hard enough time keeping my thoughts in check sometimes without all that. . . that showing." He gestured vaguely toward her torso.

Smiling widely, she drew closer to him. "Like it makes you want to kiss me again?"

"Yeah, and worse," he blurted out, leaning as far back in the chair as he could get.

"This isn't easy for me, Jenna. Man, I wanted to kiss you the other day so bad. I wanted to kiss you and more the minute I first saw you, but I'm trying not to let that old person be who I am anymore. Can you understand that?" He shook his head and sighed. "You have no idea how hard this all is for me." With a wave of his hand up and down her body, he continued, "No offense, Jenna, but girls like you don't know what wearing that kind of stuff does to guys like me."

"Girls like me?" she replied. She crossed her arms in front of her. A fire had lit in her eyes. "Oh, do tell, Parker Blevins. What do *girls like me* do to guys like you?"

"You do this girl-next-door, sing-in-the-church-choir, innocent thing with just a touch of 'come and get me.' It's kinda trashy and just plays with our heads."

"Trashy?" She threw her hands on her hips. "This better be good because you're getting yourself in deep now."

"I said 'kinda trashy,'" he answered with a grin growing wider by the second.

"Don't you dare flash that trademark smile at me, Parker Blevins," she retorted, grabbing his wrist. "That's not getting you any brownie points at all. Where do you get off calling me trashy?"

He stuck a finger from his free arm up and wagged it in her face, trying to keep from laughing. "I never called you trashy. I said girls like you are just *fronting* trashy. It's in the way you step just a little closer than you really need to when you talk to a guy, or the way you flash your eyes at just the right time. You probably don't even know you're doing it. It's in everything you do, including how you wear your little shirts with your stomach showing." He waved his hand in the air over her midsection again.

"It's hot," she interrupted. "You probably saw no more than an inch of skin showing with this shirt, so don't go saying it was trashy. I've seen much worse on a lot of people."

"See, that's where the problem is, Jenna. It shouldn't be a problem, but it is."

"Why?"

"I see that flesh, and it makes me think of the rest of your flesh," he said, releasing his arm from her grasp. He returned to the bench and rested his face in his hands. "I don't want to think of you that way, Jenna. I've had those relationships, and that's not what I want from you. That's exactly what I've been trying to stay away from."

She landed in a heap on the wooden floor in front of him and crossed her arms over her stomach self-consciously. "Geez, if you're going to get like this, just go to Michigan then." Her face was twisted into a fake pout.

"I'm sorry," he mumbled. "That was probably out of line, but I needed to say it. I made some mistakes in the past, and I'm trying to get past them. Some days, I'm not doing a very good job at it."

"I was just kidding about the kissing, Parker. I don't know. I've had relationships with a couple guys that involved a lot of kissing, but they never went further than that. I see a kiss as a kiss. It doesn't have to always lead to more." She pulled her knees up in front of her and wrapped her arms around them, resting her chin on her knee. "I'm sorry. I didn't think sharing a kiss with a guy I like was that big a deal. Just don't call me trashy."

"I want it stated for the record that I never called you trashy," Parker declared with another grin. "I so don't view you as trashy. . .actually it's the total and complete opposite of trashy. I'm really scared that *we* wouldn't work because of the stuff I've done in the past—that you would be disappointed in me and run," he confessed.

"Come on. Give me some more credit than that," Jenna Rose protested, taking his hand in hers. "I understand making mistakes. It won't be simple, but we do have to deal."

Parker smiled as their eyes met, and he nodded in appreciation.

She shrugged her shoulders, still covering her belly with one hand. "So, what's the deal with Michigan?"

"That's where my dad is. He's been a Christian for, I don't know, quite a few years now, and he and Mom think it might be better for me than living here if I'm serious about this faith thing."

"Well, are you?"

Parker kicked her with the toe of his scribbled-on shoe. "Of course I'm serious."

"Are you going to go? You can't leave us."

"If I'm not given a choice, I might. I don't want to, but I might. I'm not worried about the group. If this is the calling we're sure it is, we'll pick things up after school." His wavering confidence sounded hollow.

They both sat in silence as a group of kids on bicycles zipped past. Parker watched them in jealousy. What bliss it would be to transform back into a little kid whose biggest concern was the next crack in the sidewalk. To be a kid whose dad did no wrong and knew all the answers. He only prayed that those kids had that kind of view of life as they sped by laughing. Kids deserved that.

"How are you going to tell Dax?" Jenna Rose queried.

He shook his head, once again studying the shoes on his feet. "I don't know how I can tell him without it getting ugly."

"Ugly?"

The concern in her voice was evident. He had to remind himself that all they knew of Dax was the voice on the radio and the causes he stood for. Hiding his family from them for so long had probably created pretty bad images in their minds. Parker had never wanted them to think that a word like *ugly* would have such connotations. He determined to put her fears to rest. "Not ugly like that. He's just really opinionated, that's all, and he has a reputation that he's worried about. He's really an awesome dad, and it's been really hard keeping something this important to me from him."

"Why have you?" she asked.

"I don't know," he replied, slumping down in the chair with his hands in his pockets. "I almost think I'm afraid he'll be disappointed in me, or maybe just treat me differently. You know, I'm his protégé in more ways than one. He's had big dreams of music stardom for me. Civil disobedience and all that bucking-the-system jazz. I think he's just going to see me as part of the system now."

"What if we all talk to him?"

The idea had merit, but he had to do this for himself. If anything, he owed it to Dax. "Nah, this is what I have to do. If it comes to it, I've always got Michigan, right?"

Jenna Rose reached across and untied his shoes. Their eyes locked, and Parker once again found himself breaking the gaze. If she looked at him long enough, she might not like what she saw.

She asked, "If you go to Michigan, what happens to us?"

"Like I said, this is our calling, and the band will survive," Parker said. That wasn't what she meant; he knew that, but it was what he was hoping she would accept.

"That's not what I meant, Parker, and you know it," she replied. "I meant us. Me. You."

Opening his eyes, he found himself still on the porch with those beautiful blue eyes of hers peering into his for an answer. What was it she wanted to hear? Isn't that what guys were supposed to do in these situations—tell the girl what she wanted to hear?

Parker decided to stick with the truth. "If us being together is God's will, we'll survive the move, too," he said gently, letting her into his eyes for the first time since they had kissed.

"How do you define our relationship, Parker?" she asked softly.

With a chuckle, he threw his head back. "Wow, what a question!" Her eyes quickly told him she was completely serious.

Too many years of lying and too many years of playing girls made questions like that almost impossible for him to answer for real. He wasn't even sure if he was capable of a real answer.

"God-breathed," he replied.

"Be serious, Parker."

"No, I am! I think that's why I wigged out over that kiss."

"It wasn't much of a kiss," she laughed.

"No," he laughed with her. "It wasn't, but then again it was. I thought Christ was going to make this all a lot easier. When I told Him I was done with girls until He led me to the right one, I thought He was just going to like, take over, and that it was going to be easy sailing from now on."

She entwined her fingers in his and pulled him from the chair. "Did I ruin those plans?"

"Something like that."

Leading him to the edge of the porch, Jenna Rose sat down on the step while Parker sat down beside her. He held on to her hand and let her arm rest on his leg. "I might be a bit of a flirt at times," she said, shuffling her feet and letting her head fall to his shoulder, "but I would never intentionally lead you to stumble in your walk with Christ. If I did, I'm sorry."

"I just thought it would be more black and white, I guess."

Her smell—a mixture of coconut lotion and hair products—mingled with the summer scents as the two friends stared off into the afternoon activity of the busy street. Parker kept breathing the intoxicating smells in deeply, trying not to look too obvious. *She can keep her head on my shoulder forever,* he thought.

What did this make them—his talk, this gesture of holding hands? Did that make them a couple now?

"God-breathed, huh?" she repeated.

"Yeah."

"I guess that means no more kisses for a while, huh?"

He cocked his head to the side, letting the tip of her nose touch his own before he smiled. "I'll get back to you on that."

Being that close together, he thought she might kiss him. Actually, he wanted her to kiss him, but she didn't. And some part of him was glad she didn't.

She leaned her forehead against his and smiled, letting her eyes fall closed. He shut his eyes as well and sighed in contentment. If this girl was the one God intended for him, then they would wait for Him to dictate the timeline and logistics of their relationship. Even down to the granny kisses.

CHAPTER 223

Yah!" Elijah whooped as Parker and Jenna Rose entered the pizza shop together.

"We knew this day was coming," Andria giggled, putting her hands over her mouth and then running to give Jenna Rose a hug.

"It's not what you guys think," Jenna Rose said, sliding into the bench behind Andria. "We're still us. Nothing's changed."

Shanice reached for a slice of pizza from the half-eaten pie in front of her. "Just promise me one thing, guys." She pointed at Andria. "Don't ever get as sorry as that one is."

The two girls burst out in laughter, falling into each other's shoulders. Parker had to laugh as well at the sight of the punked-out Andria and the Barbie-doll Jenna Rose schmoozing Shanice over their friend's comment.

"Am I supposed to find that offensive?" Elijah asked.

"No, seriously," Shanice continued. She pointed a deliberate finger at Parker, Jenna Rose, Elijah, and Andria. "You, you, you, and you. Promise that all this isn't going to get in the way of our ministry. Are we a band first, or are you couples first? And what happens to the band if you break up? Where does that leave us perpetually single people?"

Parker turned to Jenna Rose, unsure of the right thing to say. Of course the band was important. It was their ministry—their work for Christ. *But what if this new relationship with Jenna Rose really is "God-breathed"?* That would make their status as a couple fairly important and necessary to pursue as well. He stayed tight-lipped, waiting for what the others might say.

"The band is always going to be the band," Andria replied. "Nothing's ever going to get in the way of that. Promise."

"Promise," Parker and Jenna Rose agreed at the same time.

"This band and what it stands for is what keeps me sane," Elijah replied. "Nothing's going to change that for me."

"And I just keep him bordered on the insane," Andria stated.

Parker passed a slice of pizza to Jenna Rose and served himself one as well. He lowered his head, her hand still in his, and offered a silent prayer for the meal. As a second thought, he asked for guidance in the building of their new relationship as well. "And help me find the strength to talk to Dax about all this," he muttered aloud to end the prayer.

He dove into the slice, not noticing the two new patrons who had entered the tiny pizza shop. The two girls took the booth behind them.

Shanice's cousin Tawny waved at the two new faces around the band's table and hurried over to the girls. Tawny and her family had lived with Shanice since the beginning of the summer, and between her job at the pizza shop and spending time at the YMCA, Tawny had found her own group of friends and was fitting in nicely in town. "Hi, Parker," she said, handing the two newcomers their drinks.

"Is the band playing tonight?" the spiky redheaded girl asked.

Tawny turned to the group at the other table. "You guys playing tonight?"

Elijah spun around and nodded. "It's not a performance, just an open practice. You're welcome to hang out if you don't mind all the missed notes."

"We'll be there," she replied. "Hi, Parker."

Parker turned around, his mouth full, and nodded to the girl. Recognizing them from the alley encounter behind Plaza Java, he gave the two a small wave as he chewed his pizza. "You guys ready to finish your autograph collection yet?"

The taller girl reached out and ran her finger across Parker's arm. "I got the one I need."

Bending out of her reach, Parker grabbed Jenna Rose's hand and gave it a squeeze. Jenna Rose winked at him, her other hand fitting tightly over her mouth to hide a giggle.

"I met them in the alley last week when I was loading up the van," he decided to explain anyway. "They wanted an autograph." He was pleased that Jenna Rose wasn't upset with the situation.

"Never asked for mine," Darby said amusedly. She crossed her arms and stole a look at the girls.

Parker shrugged and winked back. "What can I say?"

They finished up their meal and helped Tawny clean up their table. Mrs. Angelino scurried from the kitchen and shooed them away. "You get to your practicing."

"Can we come and watch?" the spiky one named Janet asked.

"Sure," Elijah said, "come on in."

Parker busied himself getting his instrument and amplifier ready for the practice as the two fans followed the group into the practice room. At other times, visitors had joined them for an impromptu show or two, and he always enjoyed their attention. But something about these two girls was different, and that bothered him. They didn't seem to care about the band or the music. Other things were on their mind.

"Dawg, if you are going to make it in this biz," he muttered to himself, "you're going to have to get used to that. Girls are going to try to get to you. You just need to get yourself in the right frame of mind to handle this."

Thanks to their local celebrity status, courtesy of their gigs at Plaza Java, Parker knew they were going to encounter some people who were more interested in their fame than their ministry. Such was human nature. He tuned his guitar and nodded at the other girl. He pondered how big CCM stars dealt with the fans whose intentions were less than honorable.

Lots of prayer, I'd imagine.

"Boy, someone got quiet," Jenna Rose giggled, bumping him with her hip.

"Aw, leave him alone," Shanice replied. "He needs to concentrate for his adoring fans."

Elijah ruffled Parker's hair. "All two of them."

"You're just jealous," Parker stated, winking at Jenna Rose.

"Man, nobody's asked for my autograph yet," Jenna Rose whined, crossing her arms across her chest.

Shanice patted her on the arm. "In due time, chick. Right now the babe magnet," she thrust a thumb in Parker's direction, "is getting all the attention."

Elijah puffed up with a wide, toothy grin. "Ha, did you hear that? She called me a 'babe magnet.' "

The two visitors pulled their chairs up in front of Parker.

Pulling his instrument over his shoulder, Parker laughed. "I think you're a babe, dawg."

"We're starting with song one, right?" Andria asked, tapping her sticks together.

Parker snatched an empty Styrofoam cup from the nearby table and heaved it at her. Instead, it floated to the floor in front of her. With a thrust of his tongue at her for good measure, he said happily, "Yeah, one. . .two. . .one, two, three, four. . ."

When Pastor Terry had met with them for the first time about being the entertainment for the community block party, Parker had floated on air for days in excitement. They were chosen in part because of a recommendation from Reverend Brinley, Jenna Rose's father.

Area pastors were asked to nominate local acts that best fit the youthful audience they wanted to attract with the musical aspects of the party, and once Second Rate was mentioned, a number of others had agreed. Pastor Terry thought they had everything they needed to provide a fun atmosphere for both the Christian and non-Christian patrons. Because of that confidence, Parker and Darby had poured over their song lists to try and put together the perfect set. They had decided on seven songs—the first, middle, and last being covers of popular Christian tunes, while the other four were their own pieces stuck in between.

Even before the controversy, they had agreed to keep the concert talking time down to a minimum.

Parker wasn't sure if that was the best option at this point. If they were going to be a real ministry, then they shouldn't be changing their show based on the venue. As he looked at the two girls watching him play the guitar, he shook his head. These girls were searching for more than the hand motions that go with "Big House."

Finishing the rousing, upbeat song, Parker motioned for the band to stop. He turned to face his bandmates. "I think we need to go back to the original show and put Andria's testimony here."

"Isn't that likely to stir up some trouble?" Shanice asked.

Parker shrugged his shoulders. "We've created enough trouble just being us, haven't we? If we're going to be a ministry, I think we need to act like one."

"No compromise," Elijah agreed and nodded his head vigorously in favor of the suggestion. He held up a hand for his friend to high-five.

"No compromise," Parker repeated.

"Isn't that going to taunt your stepdad a bit?" Jenna Rose asked. "Do you think that's the best plan? I've seen other bands just tone out the talk depending on where they're playing. It doesn't necessarily compromise the integrity of who they are."

"Maybe size it down," Parker suggested to the drummer. "Get back into the music quickly. But I think we need to keep your testimony where it is. People need to hear this."

"What about your stepdad?"

"I'll talk to him, but guys, this is bigger than him. But then again, if I'm not part of the band anymore, you guys should just do it on your own."

"We're not the band without you," Shanice replied stoically.

Pumped, Parker turned back around and started the lead-in guitar part for the second song. Janet was still in her seat, but the other girl was standing in front of him, a cell phone to her ear. His heart leapt momentarily as he heard her mention his stepdad's name in the conversation.

CHAPTER 24

I told you everything with you is about a girl."

Parker rubbed his eyes as they focused on his sister standing next to his bed. "What time is it?"

The band had practiced long into the previous evening. Parker hardly remembered coming home and crawling into bed. His headphones were still tucked into his ears as he sat up.

"Time for you to get out of bed," she replied.

"What are you doing in here?" He sat himself up and searched for his alarm clock in the folds of his comforter. "What are you even talking about?"

"There's a girl in the living room."

He threw his covers off and grabbed a pair of pants from the floor. Rubbing his head, he mumbled again, "What are you talking about?"

"There's some girl in the living room talking to Dax."

Uh-oh. Sliding his legs into the pants, he hopped across the room and peeked his head out the door. Dax was on the sofa, leaning forward, his arms resting on his knees as he spoke. Obviously, by the look on his face, he was having an interesting conversation with someone out of Parker's sight.

"What girl?" he asked.

"I don't know. Some girl looking for you. She looks like a Churchie."

"What's she look like?"

Corrina started to laugh. "She looks a bit too Churchie for you, little

121

brother. Perhaps you dissed her already and now you're trying to hide from her?"

"No," he replied in disgust. He dug a T-shirt from his dresser and pulled it over his head. "I wasn't expecting anyone. I just wanted to know who it might be. That's all."

"You're playin' again, aren't you? How many girls you got hanging this time?"

"Just go away, Cori," he sighed, pushing past her and into the hall.

"Here comes sleepyhead," Dax said, pointing down the hall at him.

Parker walked around the corner, craning his head to see who was visiting him at ten o'clock on a Saturday morning.

Jenna Rose sat in the chair next to the door. A huge smile crossed her face as she brushed a wisp of hair out of her eyes. As always, she looked fantastic in a pair of jean shorts and a fitted spaghetti-strap top with plenty of coverage. Parker smiled back.

And there's not a hint of a belly button anywhere.

"Hi," he said. "What are you doing here?"

"Just sitting here talking to Dax," she replied, "waiting for you to roll out of bed."

Dax sat back, crossing his arms in his signature stance. "Quite a girl you've been hiding here, Parker"

"Oh, stop it," Jenna Rose giggled. She gave Parker a wink. "I hope it's okay I stopped by. Dax and I are having a wonderful conversation about you."

"Well, yeah, of course," he stammered. "I just wasn't expecting you. You found your way over, huh?"

"I met you on your front step once, remember?"

Of course he remembered. That day had worked out perfectly not only for him but for the band. He had spent the day trying to think of a way to get her over to the pizza shop to introduce her to the rest of the group, when he walked out his front door to find her on the sidewalk in front of his house. At that time she had been intent strictly on hooking up with him. In retrospect, he wasn't too embarrassed to admit that he used that fact for the band's advantage. It had been perfect.

God-breathed.

"You want to do something today?" Parker asked. *Anything to get out of the house right now before he finds out too much,* he thought in desperation.

"Well, you kids have fun," Dax said, now getting to his feet. "I've got work to do today. And, Parker, we need to hang out some more, kid. I didn't even know you had a girl. It's no wonder your mom is thinking you're doing drugs or something. We don't even know you anymore." He stuck his hand out to shake hands with Jenna Rose. "It was wonderful meeting you, Jenna Rose."

Dax, you don't know the half of it.

"You, too," she replied warmly, shaking his hand.

Parker took her hand from Dax and led her back to his room. "I need to get my shoes," he whispered. "I don't want to leave you to the wrath of my sister. Then we can get out of here."

"You're allowed to have girls in your room?" she asked, taking the room's furniture in.

"You have no idea," he replied. He found a pair of blue Chuck Taylors and sat on his bed to put them on. "So, what did you guys talk about?"

"Nothing important. He's a pretty nice guy."

"Oh, I never said he wasn't. He's a great guy."

Flipping at his hair with her hand, she shook her head. "I can't believe you did this to your hair. I was absolutely in love with those curls."

"Smitten, were you?" He smiled.

"Totally and completely. That look was adorable, but this is cool, too."

He scratched his head with both hands. "It's a chop-job, that's what it is. I don't know what went through my head when I picked up those scissors."

She picked up a dusty baseball trophy from his dresser. "I can't picture you playing baseball."

"I was seven," he replied, taking the trophy and returning it to its place. "It was my dad's idea, not mine. Dameon wasn't his jock, so he had it in his head that I would be. I disappointed him."

"Sounds typical," she said with a nod.

"Dax isn't like that though."

"But you don't think he's going to understand?"

"Nope."

She picked up another trophy and looked it over. Putting it back, she faced him again. "So if he's not going to understand, what are you going to do?"

"I'm leaving it up to God. If this is what He wants of me, He'll make a way."

She crossed the room and ran a hand down his arm. "That's the best thing I've heard from you in a week. What brought that realization?"

"I don't know, actually. Well, truthfully, stressing hasn't been getting me anywhere."

"So, what are we going to do today?" She leaned against his dresser, resting on her hands and watching him.

He smiled and pulled a white knit cap over his head. "The day is yours, my lady. Whatever you'd like to do, I'm yours."

Parker hurried into the house, letting the door slam behind him. A blast of warm July air followed him in.

"What's the hurry, slick?" Dameon said. He kicked his stocking feet off the sofa and turned the television up. "Think you're late for the Rapture or something?"

Corrina rolled off the sofa beside him, howling in laughter. "Oh, you don't want to be left behind."

"You guys are both stupid," Parker replied shortly. "Where's Dax?"

"Now that's not very Christian, Parker," Dameon lectured, wagging a finger at his younger brother.

"Yeah," Corrina piped in, "what would Jesus do, Parker?"

Parker gave a deep sigh as he left the room. If this was what it was going to be like at home from now on, maybe Michigan wasn't such a bad idea. He didn't know how much longer he could handle being the butt of their jokes. One thing was certain, in his dad's perfect new life with his Sunday-school-teacher wife and two children's-choir-member kids, Parker wasn't going to have to live with taking this kind of abuse over his beliefs.

Maybe I would fit in better with Dad now.

He found Dax in the backyard, laptop in his lap. He was busy typing away at something.

"Hey, Parker, where's your girlfriend?" he called, closing the lid.

"Plans tonight. She went home to get ready."

Yeah, we're playing at our regular Saturday night gig at Plaza Java. You should come down and see us rock the place out. I might not be able to play 'Stairway,' but I promise you'll like what you hear.

"Saw her all day and more plans tonight, huh? Sounds pretty serious," Dax countered.

Parker leaned against the edge of the wooden deck, mindful of the original railing his dad had built. Being on the deck at times held its own adventure. One had to be on guard for the unsteady parts his dad had built compared to the section added on by a professional commissioned by Dax a few years later.

"I don't know what it is exactly. I've never quite fell like this before," Parker said honestly.

Dax smiled. "She like your music?"

"Yeah, she does."

"She digs your dreams?"

"Completely."

"Well, keep your head on straight. Love is a funny thing. But don't give up who you are for it. If she doesn't like you for the person you are, then she's not the one for you." He swatted at Parker with the notes in his hand and settled back with his computer.

Parker waited for the follow-up questions he knew were sure to come. It wasn't the first time he and Dax had delved into these conversations before. Generally they took that fatherly, uncomfortable turn into topics about girls and responsibility.

Instead, Dax opened his computer back up.

Here goes, God.

"I've got something for you, Dax," Parker said, pulling the CD from the wide pocket on his cargo jean shorts.

"Cool, what's this?" He took the blank CD from its case and looked it over.

"It's my band's demo. Well, it's a copy of it."

"Awesome! Got some 'Stairway' on it?" That twinkle of pride in Dax's eye brought another big smile to Parker's face. He loved to make Dax proud of him. "I didn't know you guys were ready to do a demo."

"Ah, no. No 'Stairway' on it."

"Well, I've got stuff to do this evening, but I'll put this in tonight and check it out when I can give it my full attention. Maybe I'll get a cut or two on the show tomorrow night."

"Okay," Parker said softly. He crossed his arms and licked his lips.

"You nervous what I'm going to think of it?"

"Slightly," Parker said with a laugh.

"Don't worry. You're my protégé, kid. I guarantee I'll love it."

CHAPTER 225

The rays of the late evening sun cast odd-shaped shadows on the coffeehouse floor as the band arrived. Parker hurried through the nearly empty shop to the back entrance. The chain lock was already unhooked so they could unload their equipment.

Excitement boiled over inside of him. He loved their weekly gig at Plaza Java, but this was the last night they would be merely a *coffeehouse* band. After next Friday night, things were going to be different. Thanks to the upcoming block party, the whole community was going to know who Second Rate was. Hopefully they were doing this coffeehouse as much a favor as it was doing for their band. Second Rate planned to give Plaza Java some good publicity during their stage time at the block party.

After this final hurdle with Dax, their band had no place to go but up. In his gut, Parker knew they were going to go up in a flash.

Propping open the heavy double doors, he hurried to the waiting van to help unload the equipment.

"I'm going to punk this girl out yet," Andria was saying as he joined the others.

"Who?"

"Your girlfriend," she replied. She pointed to Jenna Rose as she climbed from the van. "She's getting better, but I want to punk her out just once."

Jenna Rose was wearing a pair of faded jeans that flared dramatically at the ankle, red plastic flip-flops, and the infamous Transformer shirt that the girls of Second Rate passed amongst themselves for shows. Pulled back from her face in colorful banded twisties, her hair hung down the middle of her back in all its shimmering blond glory. Her makeup was done in her normal minimal fashion, with the addition of a glittery shine to her cheeks.

"I think I'm punked out as much as I'm going to get," she replied.

"I wouldn't tempt her." Shanice patted the blond on the back as she exited the vehicle. Her deep purple ultra-baggy pants were covered with chunky black zippered pockets, and the black Christian band T-shirt was layered with a white T-shirt underneath. Her long black hair was braided into tiny trails around her face. "She'll hold you down and do your makeup just to spite you."

"Someday you'll look like me instead of Rocker Barbie." Andria rubbed her hands together and laughed as dark a laugh as she could muster. She threw her arms open for her friends to take a good look. She wore a pair of men's blue work pants cut off at the mid-calf with rainbow-striped toe socks and Berkenstocks. A ribbed white undershirt-style tank top completed the outfit. Tipped in bright pink, her hair was spiked as usual, with her bangs parted to the side and flat to her forehead. Silver sparkle highlighted her dark-lined eyes, and she wore her normal amount of silver jewelry.

Parker just laughed and shook his head. It really was no wonder people were afraid of her. The last place that girl looked like she belonged was in anything that had to do with church.

And that was the genius of it all.

Grabbing his guitar in one hand and Elijah's bass in the other, Parker pushed past his friend and entered the building. "You are a strange one, Andi."

"I take that as a compliment," she replied.

"Yeah, you would."

The smile vanished from his face as he walked in view of the counter. Sitting at the first barstool, sipping on a soda, was his stepdad.

Dax's mouth fell open at the sight of his stepson. He turned and looked at the restaurant sign like he was making sure he was in the right place.

Parker bent down, leaving the guitars right where he stood.

Lord, be with me.

He walked forward while wiping his sweaty hands on his faded fitted jeans. The ten steps it took to reach the counter felt like a thousand, but he was determined to approach him instead of hiding any longer.

"Parker?" Dax asked, great confusion showing on his face. Parker knew by his tone that he had not entered this place expecting to see the boy he raised. He was here on a mission to save the poor youthful masses from unsuspected indoctrination. From the look on his face, he never once dreamed Parker would be on the other side. Whatever sleuth work had brought him here, it hadn't revealed Parker Daniel Blevins, his beloved stepson, as a part of Second Rate.

"Hey, Dax."

"What are you doing here?" He looked past him at the others entering through the back doors.

Jenna Rose spotted him with a gasp. She pushed Darby back outside the doors as Dax stood up.

"I'm setting up for our gig."

"Don't play with me, Parker. I came here to check out that band Second Rate and to get to the bottom of this whole thing with the block party." He took another drink of his soda. "Am I in the wrong place? A caller tipped me off that this was where I would find them."

Janet had turned him in right under Parker's nose—all while he was feeling sorry for her and desiring to reach out to fans like her.

"Well, I'm here to play like we do every Saturday night," he said calmly.

"But this is a Christian place," Dax retorted.

Parker nodded. "And I'm a Christian, Dax." He threw his shoulders back and deliberately stood as tall as he could muster. He was not going to look down at any cost. "Second Rate is my band."

Dax set the soda on the counter. His mouth still hung open, and there was a befuddled squint to his eyes. Slowly he put his hands in the pockets of his jeans and turned toward the door.

"Wait, please, Dax," Parker called out.

"You play your set," he replied softly as he walked from the building. "We'll talk at home."

Jenna Rose ran past Parker and stopped Dax before he got to the door. "Please, Dax, won't you stay and watch us play? You'll be really surprised by what you see, I promise."

Dax shook his head, rubbed his goatee, and walked past her, through the door.

It was after eleven o'clock when Parker stepped out of the van in front of his house. The windows were dark.

"You sure you don't want us to go in?" Jenna Rose asked, still holding on to his hand.

Parker shook his head. "Nah, this is my fight."

"But it involves the band," Andria stated, "so it's *our* fight, too."

"I appreciate it, Andi. But for the moment, it really is my fight. It's something I have to do alone."

Parker pulled away from Jenna Rose and retrieved his guitar from the back of the van. Usually he allowed it to stay at the pizza shop. Because they spent so much time there, and since he hated lugging it back and forth while walking, it just made sense. But he wasn't sure if he was going to be back in their practice room any time soon.

Jenna Rose stepped from the van.

Parker tried to smile, but his uncertainty showed. He was still a minor under Dax's guardianship. If Dax said Parker was done, then he knew there was really nothing he could do about it until he turned eighteen.

Elijah stuck an arm out of the sliding door and grasped Parker's hand. "We're a band, dawg."

"We're a band," repeated Parker.

"Even if we go on hiatus for now," his friend said before pulling him into a supportive one-armed embrace.

Releasing himself from Elijah's hug, Parker wrapped both arms around Jenna Rose's shoulders. He closed his eyes as he absorbed her smell and felt her breath against his neck. His flesh screamed for him to kiss her, but he wouldn't let himself do it. If this was going to be the last time he saw her for a while, he wanted the thought of her as a whole on his mind and not just the taste of her lips.

"God-breathed," Jenna Rose whispered.

He pulled himself away reluctantly and waved to the other girls in the van. Chance sat behind the wheel and was staring at the road ahead. "Later, Chance." The driver nodded.

And stay away from Jenna Rose, he wanted to say, but he knew that wasn't really fair. Chance was a good guy.

"We rocked tonight, guys," he said, thrusting a fist into the air.

Elijah yelled out into the night air as they pulled away.

Opening the door softly, he stuck his head inside first. The living room was dark and only the light above the stove shone in the kitchen. With the doorknob still under his hand, he closed the door quietly behind him and stood in the middle of the room, unsure what to do next. Should he try to find Dax and talk to him or just go to his room and wait for his stepdad to come to him?

Dax's reaction back at the coffeehouse had taken Parker by surprise. He hadn't expected Dax to look so hurt nor to confront him in public. Parker had thought it would all take place back here.

As he walked toward his room, a light from the back porch caught his attention. Snapping his fingers, he headed for the sliding glass door to face his stepdad.

Dax sat on the cushioned glider that faced the yard. Two large citronella candles burned on either side of him, sending flickering shadows across his face. His black acoustic guitar was on his lap, but Parker hadn't heard any music playing.

"Where's everyone at?" Parker asked as he slid the door closed behind him.

"Your sister is at Sierra's. Dameon's at work, and your mom went to a club with some friends," he replied, still staring out at the yard.

"And you stayed home by yourself?" Parker leaned against the railing again and planted his hands deep in the pockets of his jeans.

"Look, Dax, I'm sorry," he added, once it was evident that Dax was not going to go with small-talking his way around the subject at hand.

"Just answer me this. What did I tell you about staying true to yourself, Parker?" Dax cut back and leaned the guitar against the wall of the house before hunching himself forward and resting his elbows on his knees. "All that I told you, and you still let some pretty blond lead you around like a dog on a leash."

Turning his head away, Parker rolled his eyes. "This has nothing to do with Jenna Rose."

"From the way I see it, this has everything to do with her, Parker. You start seeing some girl, and you turn away from everything you believe? Everything I taught you?"

"Of course," he muttered in reply, once again paralyzed by the fact that everyone in his family appeared to believe the worst about him in this respect.

It was time to face this reality. *What have I honestly ever given them to think otherwise?* The old Parker Blevins was gone after he attended that concert Darby had asked him to last summer. From then on, he was buried and gone. Gone to everyone except his family. Their son had been born anew, and they were the last ones to know. He knew Dax was right to feel some bitterness.

"You have it all wrong," Parker said slowly. "I became a Christian before I even met Jenna Rose. I went to a concert last summer with a girl named Darby, and it changed my life."

"Oh, so this was all because of another girl?" Dax shook his head and sat back against the glider cushion. "Girls are going to be the end of you, boy."

Anger and frustration boiled inside him, and Parker bit his lip to keep his feelings from exploding. "No, Dax, this was all because of me, okay? I needed more to life than there was, and I found it."

"In church?" Dax chuckled and shook his head condescendingly. "Parker, I've told you over and over again about these people and the things they tell you 'you need.' I gave you the tools you needed to think for yourself. I gave you everything you needed right here." He pointed firmly to his temple.

Parker sat down next to Dax. "That's not the way it is at all, Dax."

"Well, your mom and I both think you need to take a break from all this and get your head straight again."

"You're grounding me?" Parker bolted to his feet and stomped across the floor.

"You're almost sixteen years old, so I think calling it that is a bit extreme," Dax said and picked his guitar back up. "You've got two weeks to rethink yourself a bit. Call it 'de-programming.'"

"I've got the block party next Friday!"

Dax strummed a chord and shook his head. "You've got two weeks."

They stared at each other for a moment, neither one dropping their gaze. Then, like he was signaling that the conversation was over, Dax returned his attention to the dark yard.

"This is ridiculous." Parker stormed back into the house.

"Whoa, he's still alive," Corrina said as he entered the living room. Remote in hand, she was lounging on the sofa with Sierra on the floor beside her.

"I thought you were at her house," Parker mumbled. He continued to his room without waiting for an answer. It was none of his business what his sister was doing.

The two girls followed behind him. "I thought it would be much more fun to watch you sweat. We ordered a pizza if you're interested in joining us."

"Well, I want some time to myself."

"Suit yourself," she replied. "Didn't want you around anyway."

He shut the door with a loud *thud* in her face. The gesture was rude—even for a sibling—but he found satisfaction in the deed. Crossing the room to his CD case, he grabbed the foam ball and heaved it at the door with a loud groan for good measure.

Too bad I don't have some Gaithers or good old Southern gospel. I'd play it straight for the next two weeks. Instead, he found a compilation worship CD and cranked the volume up. There had to be something on it that would irk someone in the house.

He stared at the ceiling for three songs, letting his feelings stir inside.

Flopping down onto his bed, he stuffed his arm between the mattress and the box springs. Nothing was there. Anger burst forward inside of him, and he growled into his pillow. On his feet again, he stripped his bed down and pushed the mattress aside.

"Corrina!" he yelled out.

He threw the door open in a whirlwind and tore down the hallway. Noises came from the basement. "Where is it?" he demanded as he bounded down the stairs.

"Where's what?" she asked. An open pizza box covered the end table along with a case of soda. Corrina smiled at him from her spot on the sofa, and Sierra coughed through her laughter.

"You know what. You're the only person that knew where it was."

"Just chill." She produced his Bible from under the sofa and held it up. "I just wanted to see what was so interesting about this book that you'd go through so much trouble for it."

Parker grabbed for it, but she moved it out of his reach. "Give it to me and stay out of my room, please."

"You know, you really need to work on your evangelizing."

"You're really funny," he replied. He and his sister always had that squabbling relationship, but lately, she had taken it much further than either one of them ever thought it would go. It was like she had stepped over that line from big sister to worse. And he'd had enough of it.

"You know, dude, maybe I was being serious."

Parker crinkled his forehead and threw up his arms. "You don't make any sense to me, Cori. I think I am going to head to Dad's."

Corrina shuffled her feet onto the floor and patted the seat on the sofa beside her friend. "Pop a squat. What are you talking about?"

After a weary glance, Parker sat down and gave Sierra a weak smile. She only looked thoroughly bored at the whole sibling exchange as she chewed on a pizza slice, her eyes fixed on the music videos on television.

"Mom suggested I go live with Dad if I'm serious about being a Christian. She made it sound like it was what would be best for me, but I think it's all about what's best for Dax."

"You aren't going to live with him," his sister declared.

"I'm thinking about it."

"No, you're not." She stared through him, her nostrils flaring in frustration.

"Why'd you even tell him then? You promised me."

"Think about this, Parker." She hit him on the leg. "He didn't want you when you were a skater punk, did he? No. He only wants you now because you'll be a good influence on his two little precious baby girls." The malice in her voice at the mention of her stepsisters brought a quiver to her lip. "Nah, dawg, he didn't want you until you became a Christian, and so I say he doesn't get you."

Parker pondered that thought carefully, knowing it was plausible. She was right. In the eight years since the divorce, his dad had never once suggested a move like that. Once Parker hit thirteen, his dad had even found an excuse to cancel his weeklong summer stay in Ohio to visit his kids. *I don't belong anywhere.*

"I just can't believe you punked Dax like this."

Parker shook his head and reached for a slice of pizza. "I'm just doing my thing. I wasn't expecting him to come after my big gig like this. So, why'd you tell dad about it?"

"Because I wanted to know what it was about. I just wanted to know what you had gotten yourself into."

"You could have asked me."

"Yeah, right." Corrina flipped through the pages of his Bible.

"What's with the highlighter?"

And just like that, Parker was talking about his faith and the strength he found in the highlighted notes. He shared what had brought him to the peace he now had. The words for his sister came out much easier than Parker had ever imagined. He found her receptiveness equally unbelievable.

Never underestimate my Jesus.

Parker, you've got a visitor," Corrina said simply as she walked past his door. Three days had dragged by, with Parker continuing to play loudly any Christian music he could find from his bedroom. Twice he had to go to Corrina's room to track down his Bible. He found it frustrating that she was not willing to take a stance yet. Plus, the teasing continued when others were around. Part of him just wanted to question her daily Bible reading in front of everyone, but he knew that wasn't the way to win her to Christ. He knew how extremely personal the whole process had been for him.

Planted a seed. . .

He chuckled to himself about how easily all this Christian jargon had just made its way into his thoughts.

"I'm allowed to have visitors?" he replied. "You aren't going to get me in trouble, are you?"

Dax and their mom were both at work. Corrina took her responsibility as her brother's keeper quite literally. She refused to give him the slightest bit of slack on his punishment.

"Believe me," she muttered, disappearing into the bathroom, "when you see who it is, you're going to wish you weren't allowed to have visitors."

His interest piqued, Parker cautiously exited his room and walked down the hall as far as he needed to peer into the living room.

A man standing about his height with graying hair under a Tigers baseball cap stood in the doorway, his hands in his jean shorts pockets.

He caught sight of Parker and nodded, smiling politely. "Hello, Parker."

Omigosh, Mom's kicking me out, and he's here to pick me up!

"I haven't decided I was going to come live with you." The words were barely able to make their way from his dry mouth and only escaped in a whisper. Suddenly, he felt very much like the seven-year-old boy who stood in that very spot watching his dad leave the house for the very last time.

"I know that," he replied. "I just decided to take some time to come see you guys and talk with you a bit in person. It's a big decision, I know, and I want you to make the one that's right for you."

What's in this for you, Dad?

"May I come in and sit down?" he asked.

Parker walked into the room and sat down on the edge of the sofa, his eyes never leaving the man he hadn't seen in three years—the man he was supposed to call Dad but couldn't quite bring himself to do it.

"I like this new living room set, son. It goes good in here," he said slowly while running his hand over the arm of the chair as he sat down. "It fits your mom."

"It's four years old, Daniel," Parker replied. He drew his dad's first name out as he stared at him.

I won't call you Dad. You're Daniel Chapman to me.

"Well, it wears well because it looks new." He pointed toward the hallway and gestured at the music that still blared from Parker's room. "The Newsboys, good band. I'm a MercyMe fan, myself."

The thoughts tossed and turned inside Parker's head. *You might as well give it up. That's not going to get you anywhere. Just because you know a band's name doesn't erase the fact that you walked away from your kids and my mom. None of this makes you a good dad.*

"When's your mom get home?"

Parker glanced into the kitchen at the clock on the wall. No wonder his stomach rumbled—it was nearly noon. "In a little while. Does she know you're here?"

His dad shook his head.

"She's going to wig if she finds you here."

Daniel laughed and rubbed his hands across his knees. "Well, I need to talk to her. There are things I did that I'm not proud of. She deserves to hear an apology from me. She's still hurting a lot from what I did, and I just need to try to set things right."

"So what? Is this all about making yourself feel better?" Parker demanded, the fire growing in him with every word his father said.

He pulled the hat from his head and rubbed his receding hairline. *Eek, I'm going to grow up to be bald.*

"This isn't about me, Parker," he said. "Your mom has been angry for a long time, and she has the right to be. I'm not going to deny her that, but if I can say anything that will take some of that hurt away, then maybe she'll let go of it. Seven years is a long time."

Parker stood up and stuffed his hands into his cargo pants pockets. He shook his head. "She's doing great. Dax is awesome, and he takes good care of her. If you came here to make yourself feel better, don't worry about it. She's doing just fine without your blessing."

Daniel put his hat back on his head and nodded with a defeated smile on his face. "Dax is the best thing that ever happened to her, isn't he?"

"Best thing that happened to all of us," Parker replied, staring him in the face, daring him to make a comment.

His dad scratched his head again and straightened his hat. "Can we do dinner tonight?" he asked, getting to his feet as well.

"You have to talk to mom," Parker replied. "I'm grounded."

"What'd you do?" he laughed.

"I found Christ," Parker mumbled.

Pointing a callused finger at his youngest son, Daniel's eyebrows raised in shock. "That's why you need to come live with me," he said softly.

For the rest of the afternoon, Parker whined about being mind-numbingly bored while splitting his time between PlayStation games and sneaking moments on the computer with his friends. Jenna Rose had e-mailed him, but he missed being near her. He found himself listening to their demo just to hear the sound of her voice. He was counting down the days until he was done serving his punishment.

Once he thought of leaving and got as far as the front door before stopping. "Honor thy father and mother," he muttered to himself as he stomped back into his room.

Digging another CD out of his collection, he cocked his head at the sound of a door opening from the front of the house. He dropped the CD and hurried into the kitchen.

"Hi," he said when his mom came into view.

She dropped her keys on the counter and closed the door to the garage behind her. "Well, hello to you, too. You finally over being mad at me?"

Plopping down in the chair at the end of the table, he shrugged his shoulders. "I suppose. I don't know if I ever was *mad* at you."

"You sure were acting like it." Retrieving a soda from the refrigerator, his mom motioned to the patio door. "You are allowed out of the house, you know. In the yard that is, where I'm going. I can't stand another minute inside." Parker followed her through the door to the glider. She sat down smoothly and said, "There is nothing in this world more depressing than sitting at a window all summer handing money out to people who get to go enjoy their summer days."

Parker nodded. She seemed to have a lot of those "there-is-nothing-more-depressing-than" stories when she talked about her job at the bank. He'd learned a long time ago to just nod and listen if they came up in conversation.

"You had a visitor today, I heard," she said lightly, stretching her legs out to reach the chair across from them.

"How'd you know?" he asked.

"Your dad stopped by the bank after he was here."

"He wants me to go to dinner with him tonight."

She nodded, running a finger over the can lid as she stared blankly into the yard.

"Did you talk to him?"

"He took me out to lunch." She shook her head and laughed suddenly. "Who would have ever thought Daniel Chapman would come back here and take me out to lunch?"

Parker couldn't help but wonder why she actually agreed to have lunch with her ex-husband. The fact surprised him.

"He thinks you're pretty angry," Parker said shortly as he leaned back in the soft cushion. "I told him he didn't know what he was talking about."

He followed her glance to the back of the yard where the rusting swing set still sat in the grass. A smile worked on the corners of his mouth as he remembered the snowy spring morning they had trudged outside in their pajamas and winter boots to find their Easter baskets of goodies tied to the brand-new shiny blue frame. Parker, a curly-headed blondie of all of three years old at the time, had squealed in delight and ran to the slide. After one trip down he was a muddy mess. His dad had laughed as Mom scolded him for getting so dirty. But Dad encouraged him to keep having fun, and Parker took at least thirty trips down the slide that morning.

She focused her attention on him. "He's mostly right, Parker, as much as I don't want to admit it."

"But where would we be now if he hadn't done what he did?" Parker asked. He stared at the swing on the shortened link chain.

"Up to the sky and down to the ground," Dax had chanted the day he taught him how to pump his legs. Parker had been sure he was the last eight-year-old on the planet to learn how to swing on his own, but Dax had taken care of it in no time.

Just like Dax had taken over and taken care of them over and over again in his life.

She patted him on the leg. "Not as good as we are, I think."

"So are you still mad at him?"

"Are you?"

Parker grinned and shrugged his shoulders. "I don't know what I think of him." He pulled a knee up to the back of the glider as he turned to look at her. "Do you really want me to go live with him?"

"Oh, Parker," she sighed. "I want you to do what's best for you. You're fifteen years old. You're still my baby, but you're practically a grown man. I just want you to do what you need to do."

It seemed to me during our last conversation this was about what was best for Dax, not me.

"If you're so mad at him, why do you want me to leave with him?"

She took his hand in hers and squeezed. "I shouldn't be mad at him anymore. Look at all I have now, thanks to him. I wouldn't be this happy if we were still together, and none of us would be the people we are if he was still here. I need to get over being mad at him, I know. But it doesn't mean I have to like him. He's a different man now, Parker, and maybe he should have the right to get to know what a wonderful young man you are, too."

"Does Dax want me to go?"

A tired look crossed her face as she let go of his hand and rested her chin in the palm of her other hand. "Dax doesn't even know that it's a possibility. You are so much his son." She turned and faced him, a warm nostalgic smile on her brow. "Some days, I even think you look like him. I just thought. . ." She paused as her voice cracked just the slightest.

The boy's attention went back to the swing set as he watched that curly-headed little boy in his mind play with his two daddies around the structure—the one who gave him life and walked away and the one who walked in and brought life back.

"I thought," she continued, placing a hand on her chest to regain her composure, "that I could spare him the pain of it by letting you go before he found out."

Parker tried to stifle the laughter before it escaped, but a little chuckle still got out. "I'm sorry, Mom, but it's not like I joined some cult, and I'm going to drink drain cleaner or something to get to heaven. You do not have to make it sound so dramatic."

"Well, if you were so proud of this decision, and I'm just being over-dramatic, Parker Daniel, why did you wait this long to tell him yourself? If it was something to be proud of, why did you hide it from us for so long, hmm?"

Awful good question there, pal.

And one he was ashamed to say that he didn't have an answer for.

At the sound of the doorbell, Dameon hopped up from the sofa and headed downstairs. "He's not even worth opening the door for, doof," he said shortly as Parker crossed in front of him to answer it.

"Maybe we should give him a chance," Parker replied.

"Maybe you should, but I choose to leave." Dameon closed the door to the basement behind him, leaving Parker alone in the living room.

With a deep breath and a quick motion to smooth out his blue plaid button-down shirt, he opened the door.

The first thing that struck Parker was how much Dameon resembled their dad. Shave off their facial hair, and they looked almost identical. Daniel's lines around his eyes and the corners of his mouth dug deeper into his skin than Dameon's, and his dad showed the wear of a man who worked hard with his hands. As he looked at his father's callused, rough digits, Parker was struck with the realization that he didn't know the man in front of him. He didn't even know what his dad did for a living, what he did for fun, or even what kind of car he drove.

"You ready to go?" Daniel asked.

Parker nodded and followed him out the door.

"I thought we'd head out into Amish country to find something to eat," his father suggested. "I've missed Amish dressing."

Climbing into the silver rented sedan, Parker rolled his eyes. *Just what*

I want do with my night out—eat mashed potatoes and gravy and Jell-o salad in ninety-degree weather.

An uneventful car ride ensued. Parker stared out of the window and watched the town streets turn to rolling hills of farmland. The traffic thickened as they neared the tourist areas. Parker did find himself craning his neck to get a good glimpse of the horse-drawn buggies as they passed. Mom and Dax had little use for Amish country and its home-cooked food and pricey crafts, so Parker had only been to the area a couple times for school trips.

Daniel chattered on about his wife, Nancy, and their two daughters, Ashleigh and Brittany. "Ashleigh and Brittany," Corrina would always hiss and wrinkle her face in disgust when their names came up. She predicted they would grow up to be preppy head-cheerleader snobs who looked down even on the other cheerleaders.

Once, Parker had received a photo of his two younger half siblings tucked away with a ten-dollar bill in a birthday card. Then the girls had been little blondies with curly hair put up in pigtails. They smiled widely and were bedecked in pretty pastel dresses. Having the picture arrive in his birthday card had only reminded Parker how far he was from his dad.

"I bet they get more than ten-dollar presents for their birthdays," Corrina had quipped. She snatched the picture from his hand. He had expected her to tear it up, but instead, she disappeared with it into her room.

They pulled into a hilltop restaurant and entered the building. An awkward silence began as they fumbled with the mechanics of who should open the door. Finally, Daniel stepped aside and let his son lead the way.

Seated at a table near a big picture window that overlooked the hills and an Amish farm, they both glanced over their place-mat menus.

Parker ordered a chicken sandwich after Daniel asked for the turkey dinner with extra dressing.

"So you finally decided to get rid of those curls," Daniel commented.

He folded his napkin across his lap.

His son watched him and nodded. He remembered his dad being a man who hardly used eating utensils and would often play games with his youngest son while slurping up his spaghetti and licking his fingers.

Nancy really has changed you, hasn't she? he thought humorously.

"Yeah," Parker replied, running a hand over the stiff, messy hair on his head. "I needed a change." He straightened his place mat and sighed. "You know, let's cut to the chase, Daniel. Why do you want me to come live with you now when you haven't even wanted me to visit since your other kids were born?"

"Let's talk about your spiritual walk first, Parker," he said smoothly, a quiet, calm authority to his voice that struck Parker enough to make him look his father in the eyes. That was a new change, too. "How long have you been a Christian?"

"Since last fall. Over the summer, I met this girl in our summer music program at school who played guitar. She is so unbelievably cool, and I was, like, just starstruck by her." He smiled and touched a finger to his chin, remembering that first day he saw Darby in her flowing black shirt and boot-cut jeans. Everyone else was sweating in shorts and sleeveless tops, but she had looked like a rock star without so much as a bead of perspiration showing. "Not like I wanted to hook up with her or anything like that," he added, feeling the need to clarify his intentions. "I just noticed something else about her, something just amazing that I wanted to have, too."

Daniel nodded and smiled broadly. Something about the way he responded told Parker he understood—that maybe the same feelings and questions brought his father to Christ as well.

"So, anyway, we became friends, and we hung out some talking about music and stuff like that. I'd say it was the first time in my life that I saw a girl as a real person." Parker lowered his head, focusing on the place mat.

I can't believe I just said that out loud, but if anyone should understand, he should. . .unless he's still not seeing women like real people.

"I understand completely," Daniel replied, almost as if he had read his son's thoughts. "More than I would like to admit."

"We were talking about music one day after school started, and she invited me to go see this band," Parker explained, feeling greatly relieved that he was being understood. "I went probably more to be with her than anything else, but something happened to me during that concert. I couldn't wait to talk with her about it afterwards. The music was amazing, but it was more than that," Parker continued. "The Spirit was there. I felt Him, and I finally understood what it was that Darby had that I wanted. I came to know Him then. Not long after, we were already starting to talk about our band and dreaming out loud about when we would make the big time."

"You got the music bug early, didn't you?"

Parker bobbed his head in agreement. "I could always talk music with Dax, but Darby was the first person who didn't treat me like I was nuts when I talked about my dreams. Dax has always had that dream, too, for me, but he's still reserved about it. He's always telling me I need to be prepared if it doesn't happen."

The waitress returned with their food just then. Parker's mouth dropped open as his father folded his hands and bowed his head. Shaking off his surprise at his father's behavior, he bowed his own head as Daniel thanked God for their food and time together.

Daniel lifted his head and motioned for Parker to continue as he dug into his dressing. "Oh, you can't get food like this in Michigan," he purred, chewing the bite slowly. "We have some good restaurants, but no one can make stuffing like the Amish. I'm sorry. Go on. You've been going to church without your mom and Dax knowing?"

Parker nodded. His food looked good, but the turn in the conversation took away his appetite. If he had been more open about his beliefs, things wouldn't have turned out like this. "I sneak out of the house every Sunday. No, I don't really sneak. I just leave. I didn't tell them where I was going, and they didn't seem to care."

"Do you realize how much you had your mom worried, Parker? She thought you were getting high or something. She had no idea what you've been doing."

Parker slouched back in the seat and dunked a fry in his ketchup. He struggled to remain neutral. It would be so easy to get defensive and turn this around to be about his father's failures. His face mirrored his feelings. He pursed his lips and debated how to respond.

Daniel watched him and continued, again seeming to read his son's thoughts. "But I'm not condemning you, Parker. I was a grown man with a failed marriage, three kids I didn't get to see, and a long line of trouble trailing behind me from my past when I came to Christ. I remember that initial euphoria that came with accepting Him. You feel like the world is brand new. You are all new, and you can beat anything." He swirled his fork around in his mashed potatoes as he searched to find the right words.

"The problem is those old problems don't go away. They creep back up on you, and if you don't have the right support behind you, the old flesh will take back over. If not for my church family, my wife, and other key people, I would still be that screw-up that left you and your siblings and your mom. And I think. . .I think you need to come stay with me because as a new Christian, you need that kind of support, too."

Popping another french fry in his mouth, Parker stared out the window at a horse-drawn wagon with a boy who was probably about his age, standing with the lead ropes in his hands. The wagon full of hay bales inched its way up the hillside road. The Amish teen looked back at Parker for a few seconds before nodding his head once with a smile. Parker wondered if the boy's life was any less complicated than his own given that the teen likely lived in a "simple" Christian home. He probably had his own set of issues. Just as he passed out of sight, the teen looked over his shoulder at Parker again and nodded as if he heard the wondering and wanted to say Parker was right.

"What about Corrina?" Parker asked quietly. "Or Dameon?"

Daniel lifted his napkin to his mouth. "Well, Dameon's a grown man now. I'm sure he doesn't want to move to a new state with his dad and two toddler stepsisters. And Corrina's a senior in high school. She's not going to want to come with me."

"But you didn't even try to see them today. Why didn't you invite them to come to dinner, too?"

"Well. . ." Daniel coughed slightly and picked his fork back up. "Because this visit was about you. I'd love to see them."

"Why was it all about me?" Parker asked before taking a sip of his drink. "You have three kids here you forgot about. Corrina says you only want me now because I'll be a good role model for Ashleigh and Brittany. Please be straight up with me, Daniel. How true is that? She said if I was still a skater punk like I used to be, you wouldn't be here now."

"If you're going to grow up to be a good Christian man, Parker, you need Christian role models."

"So if I wasn't a Christian now, you wouldn't be here, would you?"

Daniel sighed and dropped his napkin. "I have no idea how to raise a teenager, Parker. I wouldn't have the first idea how to be the parent of a lost kid, but I do understand what a young Christian is going through. And you don't happen to be just any young Christian. You're my son."

"So if I would move home with you and Corrina asked to come, too, you would tell her no?"

After a moment, he nodded his head slowly. "I do have two little girls I have to think of. I love all three of you, Parker, even if it doesn't seem like it, but Ashleigh and Brittany are just babies. I have to protect them. Your mom and I might have our issues, but we still have spoken about you kids throughout these years to understand the baggage that girl's got on her."

Parker snorted and dropped his fork with a loud *clunk*. "You sound like you think she'd hurt them or something. That's my sister you're talking about. . .she's your daughter." He motioned for the waitress. "I think I'm ready to go home now."

CHAPTER 28

Later that night, Parker picked up his guitar and headed to the back porch. Daniel had driven him home without another word, and they had parted ways without so much as a good-bye.

He couldn't honestly say that he had truly entertained the idea of moving to Michigan to live with his dad. There was just too much that he would have to leave behind—Jenna Rose, the band, his church family, Dax, and his mom. There was too much to walk away from simply to make *his* life easier.

Under a muggy, bright moon, he prayed and then started playing his guitar.

A short riff caught his attention, and he started to build from there. The melody was perfect for the acoustic. This was going to be another one of those psalmlike moments that would be perfect as a lead-in to a Bible reading or testimony-sharing moment in their show. With a mechanical pencil, he scrawled the notes on the lined musical tablet at his side.

"Man, I wish I could talk to Darby right now," he mumbled into the night.

Again, he focused on the riff, letting it dance through his fingers and into the darkness. A second melody came to him. He played with it and tried to figure out how to fuse them together.

"The day is gone," he sang the words as they came to him, bursting forward off his tongue. "The setting sun slips away. Gone the day. My tired soul release control to You. . ."

"That's good," he said aloud. Flipping the page, he jotted the words down.

The day is done.
The setting sun slips away—
Gone the day.
My tired soul
Release control—
To You.
I can't undo
Words I've said,
The life I've led.
Unworthy of Your gracious love
And still the love I feel
It feels so real.
My inner will
Fights despair—
How can you care
For me?
So unholy,
Imperfection,
Needs redirection.
Help me, Lord,
To wield this sword.

He read over the words on the scrap of paper and scratched his head in disbelief. "Wow, I wrote that." He couldn't wait for Darby to see this. She was sure to love it.

Throughout the week, he had talked to his friends on IM. The band had reluctantly agreed to play the show without him if it came to it, but as the week progressed, Parker was more confident that things were going to work out fine. Like he had said many times, God had a purpose for Second Rate, and nothing was going to come between them and God's purpose.

Not even Dax Blevins.

They were going to play Friday night, and he was going to be with them.

No worries.

He had spent his days since their talk avoiding Dax. His stepdad hadn't let up at all on the block party's decisions. Without naming his stepson, he went on much as before, ranting and raving about the injustices being done in the name of "family entertainment."

"You're lucky Dax isn't dragging your name through the mud," his mother said to him one day.

Parker just gave her a strange look and walked out of the room. He wasn't sure exactly how his name could be dragged through the mud over this. It wasn't like they had done anything wrong, and the general public didn't seem nearly as concerned about their status as a Christian band as Dax seemed to want them to be.

When Dax first heard the news that Second Rate was still going to be scheduled as the main entertainment, even without his stepson's involvement, he was even more determined to shut them down. Shutting down the entire block party was fine with him. He ranted every night on his show about the audacity of these community leaders mixing religion with what should have been a secular event.

A few members of the freethinkers' group had again piped in with their own thoughts to the paper and Dax's show, but the block party committee refused to budge.

The selection of the Christian teen band Second Rate stood.

Parker stared at the words of the song he had just written. Suddenly, he was ready. "It's time to wield that sword."

Parker held the phone against his ear, trying not to concentrate on how the cold plastic felt against his ear. He flipped through his mother's little phone book and found the listing for his father simply under the name "Daniel." Dialing his cell number, Parker's fingers trembled.

Lord, help me out here, please.

After the third ring, Parker started to hang the phone back on the receiver when he heard someone answer on the other side. "Dad?" he asked softly.

"Parker?" his father asked, alarm sounding in his voice. "What's up?"

"I need to talk to you better than I did earlier." He sat down in the kitchen chair closest to the phone and picked up a pen.

"Parker, you don't owe me anything," he replied.

"I can't come live with you, Dad."

"I figured as much," he said plainly. No real emotion showed in his voice.

"I want you to know that you don't have to worry about me," Parker said as he tapped a simple rhythm with the pen on the tabletop. "I may not live in a Christian home, but I have a lot of Christian support around me. I have my friends and their families and my pastor and other people at church. I have so many people praying for us because of the band, and there are lots of people willing to help us out if we need anything."

"I'm glad to hear that."

"It's not that I don't need you," Parker nearly whispered. "It probably would be easier to be a Christian if I came up and lived with you, Dad. But I don't want to be more Christian. I want to be more Christlike."

He could hear his dad breathing on the other side of the phone, and he wondered if Daniel was still somewhere in Ohio, or if he had made his way back to his fancy new house and two perfect little kids in Michigan. He wondered if Nancy was glad that he was coming home without his fifteen-year-old son in tow.

"And you don't need to worry about Dax," Parker explained. "Even though he doesn't realize it, he's taught me so much about my faith. He really taught me about thinking for myself and making decisions for myself. He's going to understand."

"If he doesn't, know you have a home here with me."

Does that go for your two heathen children as well, Daniel? Or will pretty little Nancy draw her line there? Parker bit his lip to keep from voicing the thoughts.

"Corrina's been asking questions about Christ," Parker felt the need to say.

"Is she?" he boomed from the other side. "Great! I'll pray for her."

"I can't leave now, Dad."

"No, it sounds like you can't."

"I'll call you again soon," Parker said, exhaling loudly.

"I'm going to hold you to that, and I think I'm going to come back soon. Maybe I can take all three of my kids out to dinner next time."

Parker smiled even though he knew his dad couldn't see it. "That would make us all pretty happy, I think. I'm going to hold *you* to that. Are you back home yet?"

"Not yet," he replied. "I'm sitting here in the airport listening to the radio on my headphones. I just heard a pretty cool new band on the radio."

"Oh yeah?" Parker smiled again, resting his chin on his hand.

"Yeah, it was some band called Second Rate. You ever heard of them?"

"I'll have to send you a CD," he replied hoarsely.

"I would have ordered one myself if someone was selling them on the Internet or something." Daniel laughed. Parker bit his lip, fighting back the emotion welling up in him at the change he heard in his dad's voice. "I'm proud of you, Parker."

"I'll call you soon, Dad," Parker replied before hanging up the phone.

He laid the receiver down and closed his eyes. "Thank You, Lord," he whispered. As he stared at the kitchen cabinets, he smiled as a memory of he and his dad sitting on the floor banging on pots and pans with wooden spoons flashed through his head. Mom had walked in and shouted, *"What in the world are you doing?"* over their deafening noise.

"We're practicing for superstardom," his dad had replied. "Parker's going to be the next drummer for Bon Jovi."

"Keep practicing," she had laughed. "Are you going to buy me a mansion in Beverly Hills?"

Parker couldn't remember how little he was then, but it was before kindergarten. He remembered nodding. If a mansion in Beverly Hills would make his mommy happy, he would become the next drummer in Bon Jovi.

Before his dad had fallen full force into his fantasy world, he had been a lot of fun. Parker had buried a lot of those memories under other unpleasant moments of fighting and hurt. The swing set, the silly games, even his dad's bumbled woodworking jobs—all were a part of who Parker Daniel Chapman-Blevins grew up to become.

But without Dax, I would not be me.

He had something else to do yet. He needed to make things right with Dax.

CHAPTER 29

"Hey Dax," Parker said as he opened the sliding door to the porch. A bamboo shade swayed in the light breeze, blocking the noon sun. His favorite dog-eared Michael Martin paperback in his hand, Dax was scribbling notes in a binder when Parker sat down across from him.

"You finally talking to me again?" he asked, sticking the pen in the book. He began to put the book down beside him but instead held it out for the teen to take.

Parker shook his head. He didn't need to read any more books on the atheist view. That book was actually the last book he had read before that September day when Darby asked him to go to a concert with her.

"What are you working on?" Parker asked.

"My speech for the block party protest. We've got a permit to picket on the other side of the park lane. We're going to hand out some literature and other stuff."

"I'm going to the block party," Parker said. He dug his hands into his khaki shorts.

"Oh, you are?"

"Yes, sir." He drew a deep breath and licked his lips. He was tired of lying. "Look, I could have just sneaked out, but I thought I'd be a man and tell you to your face. You deserve that."

Dax crossed his arms over his chest and settled back into the purple-flowered cushions. "So you're being a man now?"

"Yes, sir."

"And what makes you think you're a man?"

Just breathe, dawg, and say your piece.

"A man stands up for what he believes is right," Parker said firmly, balling his hands up inside his roomy pockets as he spoke. They were sweating so much that he could feel the dampness through the material. "Somebody told me that once."

Dax didn't flinch. "And this is what you believe is right? Why?" He sat back and crossed his arms. "Enlighten me."

"Well, it's like the air, Dax. You can't see air, but you can see what it does." He pointed to the moving shade. "You're never going to *see* the air. But you don't doubt its existence, do you?"

"Give me another one, Parker. I've heard the air one before." He jabbed a finger at Parker's forehead. "Think for yourself, boy. If you really believe this, you give me a reason why *you* believe it. What's this God of yours ever done for you? Don't give me jargon. Tell me from your own head."

Parker bit his lip, concentrating on the slight sting from Dax's poke.

Near the back of the yard, his mother sat on her knees digging dandelions out of her perennial bed. Parker could remember the days she would spend hours out here in her flowers. His dad would pick up the phone and head to the basement, and mom would suddenly grow old. Lines of age appeared around her eyes and at the corners of her mouth. She would head to the garden and bury herself in dirt and worms and little seedlings, all while her husband was on the phone with some other woman he had no business talking to.

Thousands of times the scenarios had played in his head. The guilt that followed him over being too young to understand back then what was going on with his parents had haunted him for years. That guilt had been the catalyst that brought him to his knees that night with Darby. He needed to be washed clean of that feeling. He also knew that night that he needed to forgive his dad. Yet even today, he was still struggling with that.

"You don't have anything, do you?" Dax asked with a smirk. "They take away your right to think for yourself, Parker. Don't you see that?"

"You." Parker turned and looked him straight in the eyes.

Lord, help me out here. Here we go.

"I learned about a father's love through a man who never had to love me or want me, but he did anyway. I believe in a God that would sacrifice anything for the children He loves because I've lived the last eight years of my life watching you do it every day." He ran his fingers through his hair and studied his stepdad's face for a reaction. "I remember how you played in a band, and I remember how good you were. I remember those dreams, and I know where you could be today. Instead, you gave it all up because you loved us enough to not think about yourself."

Dax let his eyes fall to the floor.

" 'For God so loved the world that he gave his one and only Son,' " Parker recited, " 'that whoever believes in him shall not perish but have eternal life.' It doesn't seem so farfetched when you live it. When you go from where we were to where we've become now that you're here. This family was a mess. Mom was struggling so hard to take care of us, and we were wild. You stepped in, and you not only took care of us, you taught us about love and responsibility and everything that's important to live a good life. You showed me Christ in the way you loved me every day." His eyes fixed intently on his stepdad, Parker stood quietly against the railing, his feet crossed in front of him. "God used *you* to teach me so much, Dax, and you don't even believe in Him."

The teen walked back to the door. He wasn't sure what he had expected would happen, but it wasn't this. "I'm sorry, Dax. I'm sorry that I've lied to you. I'm sorry that this was all something I thought I had to hide from you. And I'm sorry that I worried you and mom instead of being truthful. It was wrong. Most of all, I'm sorry that I've waited so long to tell you about how I feel, about what's happened to me, about what God did for me. But Dax, I have a show to do. Ground me if you want for disobeying, but I have to do this."

"And I have to be there in protest," Dax replied, still staring down at the floor.

Parker nodded. Disappointment washed through him.

God, I'm so sorry that I failed.

Parker grasped the handle of the door and looked back at his idol. His reddish hair fluttered around his face in the warm breeze as he stared out into the yard, running his tongue over his teeth in thought.

His mom, crossing the yard as she pulled off her garden gloves, winked at her son. He smiled slightly back. Her gesture put him at ease—the added stress had wreaked havoc on their already less-than-perfect relationship, and the wink said to him that all was well between mother and son as best as it was going to be.

Sliding the door open slowly, Parker shuffled inside. His stomach rolled at thoughts of living as a Christian in such an unfriendly household.

"But this is my household. This is my family, and it will all work out the way it should, because God is my Father and Christ is my Savior," he said aloud.

What he had said to his birth father rushed forward in his mind, "*I don't want to be more Christian. I want to be more Christlike.*"

Parker knew living in this house was the key for him to be more Christlike.

Sadness engulfed him as he glanced back at his stepdad once more through the screen door. Leaning against the porch rail, his mom was talking spiritedly, her hands motioning. Parker backed up from view, craning to hear her words.

"You have to admit that this is your doing, you know," she was saying. "You've pounded into his brain that he needs to live his life by thinking for himself, which means *you* have to let him live his life on his own. This is his decision."

"I know it is," Dax replied.

"So you need to let him make it. There are worse choices than this one."

Parker crossed the kitchen quickly as their voices faded away.

Opening the fridge, he grabbed a soda and pretended to be interested in the newspaper—just in case either parent came back inside.

Maybe you planted another seed, dawg. Just leave it up to Christ now.

With that thought, a peace settled over him. The secrets—all of them—were out in the open. Free of their weight, Parker's mind was clear and ready to mend some bridges and plant more seeds.

He startled at the sound of his name. Parker thrust his head back outside the door.

Dax was looking at him with a proud smile displayed across his face. "Fight the good fight, Parker."

Parker smiled back, his heart singing.

Also in the On Tour Series

the perfect girl

Jenna Rose Brinley has the voice of a star—and the looks to go with it. But when Jenna's pop-star attitude over-shadows her talent, the band wonders: *Can she really lead a group devoted to singing about God when she seems devoted only to herself?*

the backup singer

Sassy former lead singer Shanice Stevenson is content with her role, backing up the gifted Jenna Rose, in the band's exciting new dynamic. That is, until a visit from her troubled cousin raises questions of race and asks: *What is the color of friendship?*

NEW! the songwriter

True love is easy to sing about, but Darby McKennitt has no idea what it really looks like. Her twin sister has a great boyfriend, but their parents' marriage is falling apart.

Can the songwriter wade through her own con-fusion and continue to write about something she's still trying to understand?

Now Available in Bookstores

For more info about the band, sneak peeks of upcoming books, notes from the author, and more, check out www.ontourfanclub.com!